THE
Faded Flower

A NOVELLA

Paul McCusker

ZONDERVAN™

GRAND RAPIDS, MICHIGAN 49530

We want to hear from you. Please send your comments about this
book to us in care of the address below. Thank you.

GRAND RAPIDS, MICHIGAN 49530
www.zondervan.com

ZONDERVAN™

Library of Congress Cataloging-in-Publication Data

McCusker, Paul, 1958–.
    The faded flower / Paul McCusker.
      p. cm.
     ISBN 0-310-23554-5
     1. Adult children of aging parents—Fiction. 2. Fathers and sons—
Fiction. 3. Nursing homes—Fiction. 4. Unemployed—Fiction.   I. Title.
PS3563.C3533 F34 2001
813'.54—dc21   2001026582

This edition printed on acid-free paper.

Published in association with the literary agency of Alive Communications,
Inc., 7680 Goddard Street, Suite 200, Colorado Springs, CO 80920

Interior design by Melissa Elenbaas
Printed in the United States of America

01 02 03 04 05 06 07 /❖ DC/ 10 9 8 7 6 5 4 3 2 1

For Pap, in whose memory

this book is lovingly dedicated

Part One

Pap's Place

⊗⊗That day—the one when everything changed for the Reynolds family—started out as normal as normal could be. Frank Reynolds knotted his tie and tucked in his shirt as he always did, his mind pressing ahead to the day's work at the office. His wife, Colleen, dressed in the thick pink robe the kids had given her for Christmas several years before, drifted sleepily between the coffeemaker and the toaster. His son, Greg, sorted through his textbooks and notepads in a halfhearted attempt to take the right ones to his high school classes this time. His daughter, Vicki, thumbed through one of her teen magazines and wondered out loud for the umpteenth time if her parents would let her get her belly button pierced or if they would at the very least compromise on a tattoo.

There was no signal, no omen, no foreshadowing of what was to come. Everything ran like clockwork. The little moments ticked along as always.

When Colleen retrieved the day's post from the mailbox at three that afternoon, she had no idea that the beige envelope from Aunt Minnie contained important news. And Frank did not know how everything would change when he walked into his boss's office at 4:15.

But both things would forever mark the day as *that day*.

⊗⊗

FRANK STOOD IN HIS boss's office and thought, as he often had, that it looked like the set of a nightly talk show. There was the obligatory large mahogany desk and fake plants and an enormous framed photo—the size of a mural—that Frank's boss had taken years ago of some beauty spot in Hawaii. Frank's boss was named Harold Pants, and it suited him. He was a short man with bushy gray hair and had a habit of pointing at the air when he talked. (His family name, he would explain quickly, had been *Puntz* back in the "Old Country" and had been fouled up by a clerk at Ellis Island. Frank often thought that, if he'd been given a name like Pants, he would have changed it to something else as soon as he was of legal age.)

In spite of the name, Frank liked Harold Pants. They weren't friends but good coworkers and that was enough for Frank. But as Harold now paced behind the desk, his shoes swishing loudly against the carpet, Frank knew he wasn't about to hear good news. Harold was nervous. What would it be this time? After over twenty years with the company, twelve of those as head of the Personnel Department, Frank was sure he'd seen and heard it all. There were no new crises.

Frank's eye wandered to the logo of the Bradley Publishing Company that hung on the wall to the left. The logo was a "B" that rested on an open book. It had been designed in the 1950s and, Frank realized suddenly, looked like it. He had seen it a million times on the letterhead he used and never thought twice about it. But somehow, enshrined in such largeness on the wall, it looked old and outdated. In another twenty years, though, the very same logo would most likely look trendy again. Like when RCA records gave up their "His Master's Voice" logo—the one with the dog and the gramophone— and changed it to what some executive thought was a "hip" 1970s look with a pseudo-sci-fi typeface. Within a few years it looked completely unhip, and RCA went back to that dog and the gramophone. It seemed to Frank that Capitol *and* Columbia Records had made similar mistakes. Frank knew all this because he was the kind of guy who noticed record labels. He also read the entire closing credits at a movie and knew the exact contents of his wallet.

Frank suddenly realized that Harold was in the middle of a run-on sentence and that he shouldn't be thinking about company logos.

The news, when it finally came, was dropped in the middle of a long sentence like a small pebble in a large river. It was so lost in the rush of words that Frank almost missed it.

"I'm sorry. What did you say?" Frank asked.

Harold cleared his throat loudly and explained again: The conglomerate that had recently purchased the Bradley Publishing Company now wanted to consolidate everything at their headquarters in New York. Frank was no longer needed.

"What?"

"It's nothing personal," Harold said. "Just a sound business decision that you yourself would have made if you were in the president's shoes. Anyway, the severance package is generous, and there is always the windfall from the profit sharing."

The news hit him like a sledgehammer on a Dixie cup. Frank sat down in one of the burgundy leather guest chairs. "But I'm head of Personnel," he said, as if it was impossible for anyone to make such a decision without talking to him first. "If they're moving everything to New York, they'll need me for the transition."

"They have their own people to handle the transition."

"Holy smoke!" Frank said under his breath as he rubbed his chin.

Harold leaned forward and spoke in a low conspiratorial tone. "Look, I expect the Bradley Publishing Company to be completely absorbed into the larger conglomerate within five years. No one will even remember its name. Consider yourself lucky."

Lucky? Frank felt a numbing tightness in his chest like a heart attack. He'd been with Bradley since he graduated from the University of Maryland. No, before then if you counted his summer jobs there. He'd spent over twenty years rising through the ranks. And he'd expected to be there another twenty. Maybe thirty. He was a career man, a lifer. He never cared for all the moving around that other professionals did. He'd be there all the way to retirement, he had assumed.

"They can't let *me* go," Frank said, the words clicking loudly from his dry throat.

"I'm sorry," Harold said and looked at his watch. That was Harold's signal. The meeting was over.

I should have seen it coming, Frank berated himself as he walked back to his office. When the conglomerate made the offer to buy Bradley, and Mr. Bradley himself explained how it would be for the good of the shareholders to accept, he should have seen the handwriting on the wall. Except the handwriting was never actually on a wall. It had been buried in the friendly and cordial computer-generated memos that came from the conglomerate saying how no changes would be forthcoming to the personnel and how much it looked forward to working with each and every one of them into a long and profitable future. Frank believed them.

Frank's secretary looked up at him from her terminal as he walked past. "Well?" she asked. Her expression told him that she was worried. Even a strand of her red hair—always immaculately styled—fell loosely across her forehead.

He said only, "Could you see that I'm not disturbed for a while?"

"In that case, good night," she said, her expression unchanged. "See you tomorrow."

"Tomorrow?" He glanced at the clock on the wall. It was nearly five now. The day was over.

Closing his office door, he paused to take a deep breath. A clock on the single wooden bookshelf ticked loudly. Or was it the sound of his heart in his ears? He needed to think, to process what had just happened. He sat down at his desk and, clasping his hands on the armrests, pivoted his chair back and forth, back and forth. He closed his eyes. He opened them again. The office with its multiple filing cabinets and pending file holders swung before him.

How could they lay him off? Surely the company couldn't let him go just like that.

But it could. He knew that better than anyone. He was the master of the policies and procedures that dictated what happened to the employees. He could quote the rules the way some people quoted the Bible. He knew the drill, too. He needed to box up his most personal items before Clarence, the security guard, came to escort him out. It was nothing personal—just a precaution to make sure that a disgruntled employee wouldn't try to sabotage the computer system or steal important documents. Come to think of it, he was the one who had drafted that policy.

Frank ran his hands over his forehead and through his thick brown hair. It was cut short, and the gray was only now beginning to show in spite of his forty-five years. Frank yanked at his tie and unbuttoned the top button of his white Oxford shirt, something he never did during work hours. On the other side of the door he could hear the clickety-click of his secretary's fingernails on the computer keyboard. What was he supposed to do?

I have to pack. Contain the disaster somehow. Bring order to the disorder. And for a moment he remembered the morning of his mother's funeral and how he had been irrationally filled with the desire—the *need*—to reorganize the books on her bookshelf. He had arranged them alphabetically by genre. Everyone had thought he was crazy—except his father. His father had simply put a hand on his shoulder and said, "Thank you. Your mother has been meaning to do that for a long time."

Pulling a banker's box from the small storage closet, Frank started to put in the contents of his desk: the mahogany pen-and-pencil holder, the letter opener he'd picked up at a conference in Las Vegas, the photographs of his family at various stages of their lives, the gold-plated paperweight that commemorated his promotion to head of personnel. These were the collected artifacts of his twenty-two years at Bradley.

It took two boxes to get it all.

Two boxes, Frank thought miserably. *It should be more than that after all the time I've spent here.*

The clock was the last thing he picked up. It was nearly five-thirty. The soft breath of air blowing through the vent overhead was all he heard. He stood with his hands on his hips, his stomach churning. Then came a light tapping on the door. "Come in, Clarence," Frank called.

The elderly security man peeked in. Wisps of white hair floated over his head. His eyes reflected the awkwardness of the situation.

"Mr. Reynolds," Clarence said. His voice was a low croak.

"Just finishing up," Frank said with a forced cheerfulness.

Clarence shuffled uncomfortably, his patent-leather shoes squeaking like an old rocking chair.

"Can I give you a hand with one of those?" Clarence asked. He looked surprised that there were only two boxes.

Frank nodded. "The company will pack up the rest," he explained for no particular reason. "It's policy. They'll deliver anything I missed to my house."

Clarence's face flushed as he said, "It's not right, you know, sneaking you out at the end of the day like this. What do they think you're going to do, steal something? The electric pencil sharpener? The solid metal trash can? The plastic mat under your chair? What could you possibly want to take from this joint?"

Frank opened his mouth to answer, to explain to Clarence the intricacies of the policy and why it was right for the company to do it this way. But he realized with a jolt that he didn't have to defend the company. It wasn't his company anymore. "Thank you," Frank managed.

Clarence nervously jingled the keys in his pocket.

Frank grabbed his coat, his briefcase, and one of the boxes and followed Clarence out of the building. The halls were mercifully clear, as if everyone had heard the news and rushed home at the end of the day. Clarence held open the front door to allow Frank through first. Frank squinted at the September sunshine. It hadn't occurred to him that the sun might still be shining. It should be overcast and dark. And the air shouldn't be so cheerfully cool.

When the boxes had been put in the car, Clarence held out his hand to Frank. Frank shook it gratefully. Even Harold Pants hadn't offered him a handshake.

"God bless," Clarence said. "I'll be praying for you."

In all the time he'd known Clarence, Frank had never said a word about religion, though he was a regular churchgoer and solidly believed in God. Once he'd seen what looked like an open Bible on Clarence's desk, but it hadn't occurred to him to say anything. Work wasn't the place for it, Frank believed.

In the car, Frank sat behind the steering wheel and watched old Clarence walk back to the red brick building—the building where Frank had spent most of his time for more than two decades. In the years since he had first walked through those front glass doors, he had finished college, married Colleen, fathered two children, and lost his mother to a sudden stroke.

The building looked back at him with indifference. Unless an unforeseen catastrophe leveled it, that building would outlast Frank.

Frank started the car and pulled away. He didn't look back at the building in his rearview mirror, as he did every day when he left. He was afraid he might start to cry.

∞

THE DRIVE HOME NORMALLY took only fifteen minutes, since the Bradley Company was nestled in the same Maryland suburb where Frank lived. But Frank hit every red light, then came upon a minor fender bender that blocked the one main road to Frank's neighborhood. The fifteen minutes stretched to a half hour. Frank wasn't angry though. He was grateful—it gave him time to think.

As the shock of his dismissal began to wear off, Frank found himself thinking in an almost childish voice: *It's not fair, it's not fair, it's not fair.*

Being a sensible man, he reminded himself that fairness didn't have anything to do with life. So he moved on to another thought, which seemed to cry out in the same childish voice: *It doesn't make sense, it doesn't make sense, it doesn't make sense.*

Again, he reminded himself that, from a business point of view, it made perfect sense. The days of small companies were over. The conglomerations swallowed everything up and then had their way with them. Frank should have seen it coming.

In spite of his solid, practical thinking, his cry "it doesn't make sense" carried on. It became a prayer, of sorts. He did an angry drumroll on the steering wheel with his fists. This wasn't about business, this was about his life and his plans. This was about God.

All his life, Frank had made it a point not to take for granted the many good things. He had been raised to be grateful to God. And Frank was grateful. God had given him a loving wife, reasonably manageable kids, a decent living, and a secure job. God was on his throne, and the universe—at least Frank's share of it—was well-ordered, sensible, and manageable. Frank did what he could for God in return. He attended church, he was a deacon, he coached the church's softball team, he was this year's chairman of the Men's Fellowship, he tithed, he gave to the poor, and he prayed regularly and read his Bible every morning.

So what had happened to Frank at 4:45 P.M. didn't make any sense. What was God thinking? *I thought we had an understanding,* Frank complained.

Frank watched as the damaged cars were moved away and the road ahead cleared by the police. *So are you going to give me a clue about this?* Frank asked God. The car hummed, the tires rode over crunchy gravel, and God did not reply.

By the time Frank pulled into his driveway, he was rehearsing how to break the news to Colleen. "Hi, honey. Guess who gets to write his résumé after twenty-two years?" or "You're not going to believe what happened today!" or "Sit down, darling, I have some bad news." Should he tell her nonchalantly as if it didn't make any difference to their lives? Or should he sit her down, phrasing the words carefully, and assuring her by his positive expressions and light tone of voice that all would be well?

He thought of the many times he had sat across his desk from someone who had just been fired and of the manicured phrases he had used in the name of comfort. Did anyone have comforting words for him?

Frank went in through the double garage, which Colleen had left open. His fingers fiddled the doorknob in procrastination. He tried to imagine Colleen's reaction. She would be sympathetic. She would be reassuring and supportive. She would be strong. But he knew that deep inside she'd be wringing her hands and wondering what to do. He hated for her to worry. It would be so much better if he could fix the situation and then tell her after it was done.

Sighing as he opened the door, he stepped through the laundry room and into the kitchen. As always, the clean countertops looked as if no one ever used them. The appliances were in their places, as orderly as a photo in *Better Homes and Gardens*. Not a crumb was out of place. The polished hardwood floor reflected the light streaming in from the window behind the sink.

Colleen was sitting at the small breakfast table with her hands folded serenely in front of her. Her glasses and a piece of notepaper were trapped underneath them. She was in profile, gazing out the bay window into the backyard. Her light brown hair was pinned up, and she wore an oversized denim shirt. Even at this moment he marveled at how little she'd changed since he'd met her in college. The laugh lines around her blue eyes were deeper, but her face had lost none of its freshness. Considering what she'd been through with her alcoholic parents, one of whom had died slowly from liver and kidney disease, her bright looks and positive attitude were nothing short of a miracle. Frank wished he had a picture of her right then.

But when Colleen turned to face him, he knew something was wrong. She smiled, but it was a strained smile. And then it struck him that someone from the office must have called, maybe the wife of a coworker, and she already knew.

"Hi," he said. He put down his briefcase and tossed his coat over a chair. She tilted her face up slightly, and he kissed her.

"How was your day?" she asked.

Frank eyed her a moment and wondered if she was being coy. It wasn't like her. "Not the best," he said.

Colleen picked up the notepaper. "We got a letter from Aunt Minnie today."

"Oh," Frank replied automatically.

"She wants to give your father a party for his seventy-fifth birthday. She wants to make sure we'll come for it."

Birthday parties—at a time like this? He couldn't think about it now. And Colleen would understand why in a minute. "We'll see." He opened the refrigerator to find a drink. His mouth had gone dry.

"That's not all," Colleen said in a level voice. "She wants us to come for another reason."

"Oh?" Frank asked again, feeling more confused. Maybe he should just blurt out the news so Colleen could see how unimportant Aunt Minnie's letter was.

"Aunt Minnie thinks your father has Alzheimer's disease."

Frank began his unrehearsed speech. "Colleen. . ." And then he did a double take—an honest-to-goodness, straight-from-the-movies double take. You could almost hear the wagga-wagga sound like they made on *The Flintstones*. "What?"

She held up the letter. "It's all in here. He's been showing the symptoms for the past few months, and Dr. Janssen thinks they're getting worse."

Frank took the letter and glanced at his aunt's neat Peterson-method cursive writing. "She actually persuaded him to go to Dr. Janssen?"

"They're worried he'll hurt himself if he's not put into some kind of care. She wants us to come and talk him into it."

"Into what?"

"Going into a retirement home, or assisted living, or whatever they call those hospitals now."

"Move out of his house?" Frank was already shaking his head. Not his father. He wouldn't do it in a million years.

"She says he can't live alone anymore. It's not safe."

Frank opened a can of soda. It spat and then suddenly sprayed all over him. He shouted and held the can away from him like a hand grenade as he raced to the sink. He dropped it with a hiss, fizz, and clatter.

Colleen grabbed some paper towels, wet them, and wiped up the floor. Frank picked up a hand towel to clean himself off.

With his back to her, he said, "I guess this makes the perfect end to a perfect day."

"I'll take your suit to the dry cleaners tomorrow."

"I won't need this suit tomorrow. Or even the day after that. They fired me today."

Frank turned to face his wife, trying to anticipate her reaction. But she didn't react. At least not the way he thought she would. She stood frozen in the middle of the kitchen floor, clutching a soda-saturated paper towel.

"You're kidding."

"Nope," he said.

Colleen laughed. A giggle at first, and then a full-blown laugh with her head tilted back.

Frank couldn't have been more puzzled. "Did I miss something?"

"I had lunch with Sally today," Colleen said, when she had herself under control.

Spooky Sally from church, Frank remembered. She was the one oddball member of their church who seemed to have visions and messages she called "words from the Lord." She gave Frank the creeps.

Colleen continued. "Sally told me she had been praying for us. She said she suddenly got a 'picture' of us moving away from here and living in your father's house. I thought she had gotten her wires crossed. I couldn't imagine how such a thing would be possible." Colleen giggled and then erupted into full-blown laughter again.

Frank was mystified. He didn't see anything funny about it at all. "Colleen?"

Colleen lowered her head and waved him away, still laughing. She put her hands on the serving island in the center of the kitchen, with her head down. And then her shoulders started to heave and the laughter became hitched with sobs, and Frank went to her.

"But I hate hospitals," she choked out.

Frank embraced her from behind, remembering what she'd gone through with her father. "I know," he said and then closed his eyes. He breathed deeply and could smell just a hint of flowers in her hair.

∞

THE REYNOLDSES HAD A family meeting in the dining room over supper. Frank studied his two children as they sat down. Greg favored Colleen's side of the family, with their fair features, large eyes, pixie-like noses, and light brown wavy hair. He was a heartbreakingly handsome boy except for the trendy goatee, which, in Frank's opinion, looked silly. However, Frank's biggest worry for Greg was that he spent too much time with his computer and not enough with flesh-and-blood people.

Vicki got her looks from Frank's side of the family. There were times when she looked uncannily like Frank's mother. She'd flick at her black hair or tilt her head in such a way, and Frank would be transported back in time to his childhood, when his mother still had her youthful features. Vicki also had his mother's dark eyes and an aquiline nose that made her face look longer than it was, and she had a distinctive dimple to the right of her mouth. Like most girls on the edge of adolescence, she had her mood swings, but for the most part, she was good-natured and friendly. Both of his kids were.

Frank had learned over the years that it was best to be direct with his kids, so he was. He told them he'd been fired that afternoon.

At first they were speechless. Then Greg shook his head and said, "That stinks. Just what I'd expect from big business. There's nothing personal, there's no humanity..."

"Are we going to have to move?" Vicki asked.

Frank, who didn't really know the answer to the question, replied, "No, I don't think so."

Vicki frowned. "But I want to move away. I'm really sick and tired of Melissa."

"But she's your best friend," Colleen said. "You'd miss her if we had to move."

"No, I wouldn't," Vicki said.

Greg snorted and rolled his eyes.

Vicki elbowed him. "I wouldn't! She's always teasing me because I'm not allowed to get my belly button pierced."

Frank eyed his daughter wearily. "You're going to bring that up at a time like this?"

Vicki shrugged, but a wry smile crossed her face.

"I think it's the best thing that could happen to you," Greg said to Frank. "Now you can break free and do what you *really* want to do."

"I was doing what I really wanted to do," Frank said.

"You're kidding, right? You didn't really like your job."

"Yes, I did."

"You're just saying that because it's what you got used to. I mean, how could you like sitting behind that desk day after day?"

Frank gazed at his son with disbelief, his hand and fork frozen in midair. "You, the one who sits at his computer for hours on end, are going to complain about *my* sitting at a desk?"

"We're not talking about me right now, we're talking about you," Greg said, undaunted. "Just look at the garage, Dad. All those tools and machinery around your workbench. Isn't that what you really like to do? Make things? Isn't that what you spend every available weekend doing?"

"It's a hobby, Greg," Frank explained in a measured tone. "One day you'll understand the difference between a job and a hobby."

Greg shoved a forkful of mashed potatoes into his mouth. "I hope not."

"I don't want to talk about this now," Frank said with a groan. "You better give them the rest of the news," he said to Colleen. He helped himself to another spoonful of green beans. His hands were shaking so badly that he dropped a couple of them on the way to the plate.

Colleen told the kids about Aunt Minnie's letter.

"A party would be cool," Vicki said.

Greg looked at her indignantly. "Didn't you hear anything beyond the word *party?* Pap is sick. He's got Alzheimer's disease."

"Do you know what that is?" Colleen asked Vicki.

"Sure I do. It's when you forget things." She then smiled at Greg. "I guess *you've* had it most of your life."

Greg let out a sarcastic laugh.

Colleen folded her napkin and placed it next to her plate. "So what's our plan?"

"Plan?" Greg asked incredulously. "What kind of plan do we need? We have to go to Pap's party."

"And Dad has to find a job," Vicki added.

"Or maybe Dad won't get a job, and we'll all move in with Pap, just like Spooky Sally said," Greg speculated.

Frank shot Colleen a disapproving look. He really wished she hadn't told them about that.

"What about your college?" Colleen countered. "There isn't one anywhere near Peabody."

"Who cares?" Greg said. "I think college is overrated anyway."

Frank, who'd been folding and refolding his napkin, looked up. "I suppose you're going to pursue one of your moneymaking *hobbies?*"

"Sure. Why not?"

"Which one in particular will make your fortune?" Frank challenged him. "High scores on one of those computer games? Or maybe you'll rake in a lot of money from spending hours in those Internet chat rooms."

"It could happen," said Greg.

"No, it couldn't," replied Frank. "I've spent a lot of my career dealing with people who didn't have college degrees and were stuck in their jobs. They couldn't go any further up than they were. You *need* a degree to get anywhere in business."

"You mean like you did?" Greg snapped back. "Yeah, right. Look where your degree got you."

There was a collective intake of breath between Colleen and Vicki. Stung, Frank simply stared at his son.

Greg lowered his head and pushed his fork around his plate for a moment. "I'm sorry. I didn't mean it," he eventually said.

"Yes, you did." Frank got up from the table and took his dishes to the kitchen. At the sink, he thought: *The whole world is against me. It's a conspiracy.*

∞

IN THE TWO WEEKS leading up to the trip to Peabody and Pap's party, Frank sent his résumé out to every contact he had. He waited a couple of days and then phoned his contacts directly. They were all aware of his situation but had nothing to offer him at the moment.

It was Brad Meyers, an old friend from another publishing house, who put it in perspective: "You're too old to hire."

"I'm only forty-four!"

"You're forty-five. And in our business that makes you too old." Bill sipped his brand-name coffee. "Why pay you what you're worth when there are younger, more enthusiastic people they can hire for less money?"

"Doesn't experience count for anything?"

"Not as much as we experienced people like to think."

"Then what am I supposed to do?"

"Try one of the New York companies."

"I don't want to go to New York."

"Then I don't have an answer for you."

It was soon after that conversation that Frank began to wake up in the middle of the night, unable to breathe. It was as if the room had simply run out of air. And once he was awake, his mind went through all of the worst possible options for his future. They might have to sell the house. He might have to take a job at a fast-food restaurant, working next to his daughter's friends. Or Spooky Sally might be right after all. He'll end up living back in Peabody again.

He went to the garage on those sleepless nights and started to build a bookcase. He didn't know who it was for, but he wanted to build it anyway. Maybe it was the one thing in his life that he could control. The wood would not surprise him. The saws, the bits, the lathes—none of them would let him down. With his guidance and control, they did what he needed them to do.

Colleen, meanwhile, coordinated the birthday party with Aunt Minnie. Minnie, who was Frank's mother's sister, was thrilled that they were coming up. And somehow they always seemed to avoid any discussion about Pap's condition or what had happened at Frank's job. That was something for Frank to work out.

"What about Dennis?" Colleen asked Frank one evening. Dennis was Frank's older brother who was now living overseas. "Aunt Minnie thinks it'd be wonderful if he could make a surprise appearance."

"Fat chance," Frank replied. Dennis had left home years before, initially taking a job in the Gulf with an oil company. After that he had worked in Europe for a bank with an unpronounceable name. Now he was in Korea, managing a firm that made computer parts. Or something like that. Frank wasn't sure, and Dennis was always vague about it.

"You should at least call him so he knows about it."

Frank grudgingly agreed. But he knew the outcome even before he'd finished dialing the dozen numbers on the phone. His brother was pleasant, cordial, sympathetic, but didn't think he could come back unless it was a genuine emergency.

"In other words, don't call you unless he kicks the bucket," Frank said.

The line hissed for a moment. "You don't have to be like that."

"We were hard-pressed to get you back for Mom's funeral."

"That wasn't my fault."

"Then whose fault was it?"

The line hissed again. "Look, there's nothing I can do to help now, right? You've got everything under control. Just call me if things get bad."

"Yeah, I'll be sure to do that. Oh—and I forgot to tell you that I was laid off the other day." Frank hung up.

The phone rang immediately, and Frank wondered if Dennis could have dialed so quickly. Frank picked up the receiver, but it wasn't Dennis. It was Pap.

"So when are you coming up?" he asked. These were always his first words after "Hello."

"Oh, I don't know. Sometime soon, maybe."

"My birthday's just around the corner, you know."

"That's right. I better remind Colleen to send a card."

"Send yourselves. Come on up."

"Okay, Dad."

"How's work?"

Had Aunt Minnie mentioned to Pap what had happened to Frank? "Things are a little quiet right now," Frank replied.

"Good. Then you should be able to come up."

"Okay, Dad," Frank said as finally as he could. "How are *you* doing?"

"My knee's been a little stiff lately, but I think that's because we're going to have an early snow."

"October is too early for snow in Peabody."

"Is it October already?"

"Uh-huh."

"I don't know where the time goes. You know I have a birthday right around the corner."

"Yes, Dad, you just said that."

"I did?"

Frank said he had and was suddenly conscious of the many times his father had repeated himself. Were these symptoms there all along, and he hadn't noticed before? How many times did his father tell the same story of something that had happened in town? Or how many times had he mentioned that the same person had died? Or his struggles with the flowers in the garden? Or some other trivial bit of information?

"Are you still there, Frank?" Pap asked.

"I'm here."

"Did you hear the one about the drunk who was about to go into a bar? A street preacher stopped him and said, 'Stop, friend! The devil is in there!' The drunk slurred, 'Well, if he is, he's buying his own drinks!'"

Frank laughed politely, though he'd heard that joke from his father more times than he could count. This was how his dad said good-bye.

"I'll talk to you soon, Dad."

"Good night, Son."

Frank hung up. He felt a deep disquiet. He didn't know much about Alzheimer's and needed to do some homework. Maybe he should call Dr. Janssen. If he could get a few answers, then he would know how to deal with this problem.

As the days passed, Colleen bought several books about the disease. She summarized for Frank how Alois Alzheimer, a German physician, had been the first to describe it early in the twentieth century. Nowadays it was called *senile dementia–Alzheimer's type*,

The Faded Flower   24 or SDAT. After heart disease, cancer, and strokes, Alzheimer's came next on death's hit parade. And at the age of seventy-five, Pap was in the 1% group of the population who suffered from it. Percentages increased with age.

It attacked the brain, Colleen explained, reducing memory, altering judgment, affecting language, diminishing motor skills, and changing personality. Paranoia was common among patients. Maybe it's genetic, maybe not. Maybe it had to do with proteins, maybe not. What the experts didn't know about it seemed greater than what they did. Frank listened attentively, but couldn't bring the facts together with the picture of the father he'd known all his life.

∞

GASPING FOR AIR, FRANK sat up in bed.

Without turning on the light, Colleen moved next to him and took his hand in hers. When he'd got his breath back, she said, "Maybe it's because we don't pray together anymore."

"Maybe it's because you tell me Alzheimer's stories every night before I go to sleep."

"We're under a lot of stress right now. We should pray, Frank."

"I guess we should."

"But you don't really want to."

The truth was, Frank didn't. He'd lost his job, and he seemed to be losing his father. Where was God in any of it? And even if God was around, what could he do about it? Find Frank a job? Frank never imagined God as an unemployment genie. And what about Pap—would God miraculously heal him from Alzheimer's? Probably not. Why would God do that for Pap when he doesn't do it for any of the other millions who are stricken with the disease? But Frank didn't say any of that to Colleen. He didn't dare admit that he hadn't really prayed since the day he was fired. He knew she'd come back with answers like, "But God loves us" or "He's in control"—answers she truly believed but Frank wasn't sure about right then. So Frank chose the diplomatic route and said, "You pray for us."

Colleen did. And as the words came softly from her lips, Frank thought of Clarence who, if he kept his word, might be somewhere doing the same thing right now. Frank wondered if a barrage of voices might move God to action.

Probably not, Frank thought. *This is my problem to fix.*

The morning they were to leave for Peabody, Spooky Sally stopped by. "I'm so glad I caught you," she shouted as she climbed out of her car. She was a heavyset woman who puffed and panted as she raced up the driveway, her red hair flying wildly around her as if it had weather all its own. "You have to hear this!"

Colleen smiled pleasantly and invited her in for a quick cup of coffee. Greg and Vicki seemed to disappear. Frank was suddenly sorry that he'd finished packing the suitcases into the car. Standing with his hands in his pockets, he tried in vain to think of something else to do.

"Sit down, Frank, you need to hear this," Sally said.

Colleen tipped her head towards a chair. There was no escape.

Sally looked at him earnestly for a moment. Her round face was smothered in makeup. Her lipstick was a bright red, and she wore too much black mascara on her eyelashes. There was no other word for it, Frank thought. She's spooky. And he felt like she was about to read his palm.

"I had a picture last night while I was praying," she finally said, her eyes fixed on Frank. "I saw you sitting in a small windowless room."

"Oh?" Colleen asked.

But Sally kept her gaze on Frank. "You were at a table, carving a piece of wood. Directly in front of you was a heavy iron door."

"You've seen my office at work," Frank quipped.

"Be quiet, Frank," Colleen said.

Sally continued. "Suddenly a key was pushed into the lock on the door. With heavy clicks and clanging and the sound of latches being drawn and rusty hinges being brought to life, the door opened. Bright light poured in. You winced and covered your eyes. A figure stood framed in the doorway."

Frank opened his mouth to speak, but Colleen laid a hand on his arm.

"The figure spoke to you," Sally went on. "'You said you'd follow me,' the figure said to you. But you pretended not to understand. Then the figure said: 'Follow me now.'"

"And I did," Frank said, hoping to bring the curtain down on her picture.

"No!" Sally said. "You knew who it was, but you looked down at your piece of wood and asked, 'Follow you to where?' And the figure said, 'To freedom.' You kept looking at your piece of wood and asked, 'What kind of freedom?' 'Come and see,' the figure replied." Sally sat back and closed her eyes.

Frank felt a little embarrassed for Sally and her performance. But for Colleen's sake, he waited patiently.

Suddenly Sally sat forward, her green eyes wide. "You moved as if you were going to get up and leave. But instead you looked around at the room—your cell. How could you leave this? It was safe, you reasoned. It was home. And the light outside was so bright. Maybe if you could see what you were trading this room for, then maybe, just maybe. . . . So you asked, 'Will you give me some idea of where you want to take me?' The figure receded, leaving only the light, and then the door closed again. You went back to working on your carving as if nothing had happened."

Frank was alarmed to see that Sally's eyes had filled with tears. She pulled a handkerchief from her sleeve. "I haven't seen a sadder picture in all my years," she sniffed and blew her nose.

"It's a little *unsubtle* for a vision, isn't it?" Frank observed.

"They're not *visions*," Sally said. "They're only pictures. And it isn't for me to say what it means. You need to figure that out for yourself."

"Okay, thanks," Frank said and made as if to stand up.

Sally reached for his hand and said urgently. "Frank, don't lock yourself in."

Frank put on his head-of-personnel smile. "I won't, Sally. Don't worry."

∞

THE DRIVE TO PEABODY took them through beautiful rolling hills, rich farmland, and forests that were now exploding with the yellows, browns, oranges, and reds of fall. Frank loved the drive from Maryland to Pennsylvania, not for the destination itself, but for the sheer beauty of traveling there.

Peabody was nestled at the base of a mountain—Mount Summit—that boasted a ski resort, a large lake filled with trout, and the scars of strip-mining. Peabody itself was the gateway from the mountain to a stretch of country with gently sloping hills. Downtown had only one building that was over five stories tall: the Peabody Bank and its offices. The rest of the area was made up of shops, cinemas, department stores, and local offices for insurance agents, mortgage brokers, doctors, and dentists. The downtown district had gone through a terrible upheaval when the mall was built on the outskirts, with businesses closing down, windows boarded up, and the streets left derelict. Frank had heard, though, that a local entrepreneur was determined to revitalize "Old Peabody" and return it to its former glory. Or something like it.

There was more than enough of "Old Peabody" for Frank's tastes. The buildings and familiar neighborhoods that were left were enough to make him feel as if he'd entered a time warp and had been transported back to his past. "Just call me Marty McFly," he said to Colleen as they entered the city limits.

Colleen had once observed that, for her, it wasn't going *back* to the past as much as it was the *past coming forward* to meet them. Either way, Frank didn't like the feeling. He had worked hard to break free of the small-town mentality that he believed threatened his future. Unlike most of his high school classmates who had wound up getting jobs in the area and staying there, Frank had saved to go to college; he had escaped from what he viewed as the oppression of small-town despair.

Returning to Peabody brought all of those feelings back. Peabody was haunted, a town full of memories that walked like ghosts among the living.

As clear as day, Frank saw Mrs. Emmerson, who had been his Sunday school teacher at the little Methodist church. She'd been ancient then, surely she was dead now. But there she stood in the doorway of the church, flapping a paper fan that spread out into a picture of Jesus. "Straighten your tie," he could hear her saying with a breath that smelled of lozenges and a large smile that came from dentures that were too big. The boys in the class had a yearlong debate about whether or not she wore a wig until Mike Janowsek ended it by confessing that he'd seen her without her hair one Saturday morning when he mowed her lawn. "She's bald!" Mike gasped.

And how could he drive past Rudy's Tastee-Whiz without seeing Old Mr. Rudy, white paper cap on his head and stained apron around his waist, standing like a wizard at the green-and-chrome milk-shake maker? But Frank knew Old Mr. Rudy had been dead for years, and the recipe for the best chocolate shakes in the world had gone to the grave with him.

But the ghost Frank saw the most was his mother. He saw her standing in line at Greene's Grocery, where the front was made of tent flaps and the inside was always thick with the smell of vegetables in spite of the enormous and ancient soot-covered fan that pretended to blow fresh air into the shop.

And there she was walking into Kendall's Pharmacy. Or waiting to get tickets for a show at the Coliseum. Or strolling down State Street with a Hayes Department Store shopping bag on her arm, her face young, and her hair tucked under a pillbox hat.

THE REST OF THE family also saw ghosts of memories as they drove through town towards Pap's place. Colleen saw Frank's mother, but as an older woman, the one who became a loving mother-in-law and a doting grandmother. She appeared to Colleen as they drove past Memorial Park, near the statue of the soldier from World War I where, on more than one occasion, she had chased little Greg and given ice cream to baby Vicki.

Greg saw ghosts of old family members near the pavilion behind Peabody High School, where they had gathered once a year for the big Reynolds/Malcolm reunion with distant uncles, aunts, and cousins. Greg saw them all now, as he'd seen them then, leaning over red-checked picnic tablecloths covered with fried chicken, potato salad, and home-baked bread that was still warm and smelled of heaven. He heard their voices and saw their bobbing heads of trussed-up hair and old hats. And at nightfall, when the food and the horseshoes had been exhausted, Greg and his cousins caught lightning bugs that winked at them with little green lights from empty preservative jars with holes in the tops.

For Vicki, the only ghost was Pap himself, though a younger Pap than she would see today. His ghost had a slender, unwrinkled face and less hair on his ears. She remembered him sitting in his favorite chair, making faces at her or reading her a story. He had shown her how to color within the lines of her coloring book by tracing everything in black first. He had taught her to play Chinese checkers. He had given her rides on his back like a horse. Together they had sat at the old player piano down in the basement, even though she'd been more interested in the various levers and the way the piano keys moved by themselves than in the music it played. As the sun set, they'd ridden the glider on the porch, back and forth, back and forth, and listened to the crickets that sang somewhere beyond the fat white blossoms that grew wild next to the garage.

At least three of the Reynolds family welcomed the memories and embraced them for the treasures they brought. Frank alone would have avoided them if he could. His memories brought with them a feeling of longing—but a longing for what, he couldn't say. Maybe it was despair disguised as longing, a longing he knew he could not fulfill. And why indulge the memories or the longings they created? It wasn't as if going back to other times could ever solve any of today's problems. The world spun on, and there was nothing anyone could do about it. That was the singular lesson Frank had learned when he'd lost his job.

∞

PAP'S PLACE SAT ON the corner of Braddock and Charles Streets and remained a testimony to an age gone by. Pap still had a windmill in the middle of the rock garden and a politically incorrect figurine of a black stable boy holding a lantern by the front door. The house was three stories tall, plain and boxy with white aluminum siding and black shutters. Untrimmed bushes threatened to rise above the windows in the front. And an elm tree cast shade over half the back. The entire plot of land was encased by a short white picket fence that now leered at them with broken teeth.

"Something else to fix," Frank said as they pulled into the gravel driveway. He stopped behind Pap's Dodge, which sat halfway in the freestanding garage. There was a dent in the rear right fender as if he'd narrowly scraped past something. Probably another car.

"Is he going to be different?" Vicki asked from the backseat.

"I don't know," Frank answered via the rearview mirror. But it was the first time since the kids had been told about Pap's condition that he'd heard any anxiety in Vicki's voice.

Colleen half-turned in her seat. "He probably won't look different, but he may act different. Alzheimer's is unpredictable at this stage."

Dead leaves lay scattered on the front porch, the wind gently prodding them to the corners and under the rusting metal glider and into the rotting slats. The screen door banged against the frame. The inside door was open.

"Pap!" Frank called out as he entered.

Colleen followed and observed, "It still smells like pine needles."

"And it looks even more like a junkyard," added Frank, surveying the cluttered living room. Pap was an Arabian merchant at heart. He bought things he didn't need just in case someone he knew might want one. The junk—things like old radios, Philco televisions, old helmet-style hairdryers, and record players—were usually kept in the basement and brought in or taken out through the double coal doors. But now Frank saw that the infestation had moved upstairs. Three televisions of various sizes and shapes now sat in the living room. An old Underwood typewriter, along with something that looked like a telegraph, sat on the end table.

Greg chuckled. "And you complain about *my* room."

From the kitchen Colleen cried out.

"What's wrong?" Frank called to her.

She appeared in the doorway. "I'm going to have to buy some rubber gloves and give this place a *deep* clean. You can't see the sink through all of the dishes. Does anyone want something to drink?"

Everyone did.

"Pap!" Frank called out again. There was no answer.

"I'll see if he's upstairs," Vicki said and darted away.

Still looking at the living room, Frank stood with his fists clenched under his armpits and felt sick at heart. "This was a mistake. We should have told Aunt Minnie to bring Pap down to us for his birthday. This town, this *house*, makes me feel like I've walked face-first into a roomful of cobwebs."

"Gripe, gripe, gripe," Greg teased. "I don't think there's anything wrong with this town *or* this house." He dropped on the couch, then instantly hiked his butt up. He felt underneath and retrieved a Ping-Pong paddle.

"He must be out," Vicki said as she bounded back down the stairs. "He's not upstairs."

Frank wondered if he should check the basement.

"Can we go to the mall later?" Vicki asked, slinging herself over the arm of a chair. "I want to see if they got any new stores."

"Aunt Minnie said they've opened a new Hammond Organ shop," Colleen called from the kitchen.

"Then what are we waiting for?" Greg said with feigned excitement.

"Did you see all the funeral homes on the way in?" Vicki asked. "I never noticed so many before."

"One on every corner," Frank said. "Maybe that's a business I should get into."

"I saw one with golden arches and a drive-up window," quipped Greg. "You could order lunch during the viewing."

Colleen reappeared in the doorway with an open can of dog food in one hand and a bottle of floor wax in the other. "Why do you think these were in the refrigerator?"

Vicki jumped up, excited. "Do you think he got a dog?" She began to search the house, calling "Here, poochy" as she went.

"He can't take this junk with him," Frank continued. "No convalescent home could hold it all."

"Why not ask him to come live with us?" Greg asked.

"Don't start, Greg. We talked about that. For one thing, if what Aunt Minnie says is right, he'll need professional care. For another thing, we may not have a house for him to live in if I don't find a job."

Colleen frowned. "We don't have to talk about this now, do we? We're here for his birthday. We're going to dress up in costumes, have cake and ice cream, and make a night of it. It'll be a nice celebration. We can deal with all the serious things afterwards."

"Costumes? *What* costumes?" Frank asked. He and Greg exchanged worried looks.

Colleen continued from the kitchen. "Minnie and I decided to make it a costume party. We thought we could dig through the boxes in the attic and dress up. You know how your father loves that sort of thing."

"You're kidding."

Colleen looked back out from the kitchen doorway. "Frank, we didn't drive all this way just to brood or argue. We're going to celebrate. It's not every day that a man has his seventy-fifth birthday. It's a milestone."

Millstone, Frank thought.

Vicki returned from her search. "No dog," she announced. "But if you think *this* room is bad, just wait until you see the rest of them."

There were four large bedrooms on the second floor, and the attic had been converted into a fifth bedroom for Greg and Vicki, or Dennis's three kids, depending on who was visiting. Greg claimed the attic; Vicki went into what had once been Dennis's bedroom. Frank and Colleen put their things in Frank's old room. A mustiness filled the air.

Colleen started to put some of their clothes in the tall chest of drawers.

Frank sat down on the bed. The springs screeched. "If we can get Pap to agree to move into a home, do you have any idea what it'll take to sell this place?"

"It'll get a good price, won't it?"

"I mean getting it ready to sell, cleaning it up."

"What if we don't sell it?" Colleen asked with a smile. "Remember what Spooky Sally said."

"I'd rather not, thank you."

Colleen gave him a couple of shirts to hang up in the closet. It smelled of mothballs, and the rack wobbled as if it might come loose from the wall. At the bottom of it was a square hole that served as a laundry chute to the basement. Frank suddenly remembered that as a boy Dennis had fallen down that chute. His fall was broken by the pile of laundry that had gathered at the bottom, and he only had a few scratches and bumps. But from that time on, Frank stayed clear of the laundry chute. Its black hole was more menacing than any imagined closet-monster.

Frank glanced at his watch. They'd been there half an hour and still no sign of Pap. Should he be worried? Didn't Alzheimer's sufferers often go strolling off on a simple errand and then forget who they were and where they lived? Frank could tell by Colleen's face that she was thinking the same thing. Should he go looking—or call the police?

"I think I'll call Aunt Minnie," Colleen said lightly, as if she wanted to talk about the party. But Frank knew better.

∞

AUNT MINNIE WASN'T AT home. But the moment Colleen put the phone back into the cradle, the front door opened and in walked both Pap and Aunt Minnie. They carried grocery bags.

"Hello!" Pap called out.

"We were getting worried," Frank said.

Pap slid past him to the kitchen and smiled smugly. "I knew you wouldn't miss my birthday."

Aunt Minnie kissed everyone as she always did. She smelled of her favorite perfume. Frank smiled at her. Though she was over eighty, she looked younger, mostly due to her good health and her sharp fashion sense. No old people's clothes for her. But what always startled Frank were her classic Malcolm eyes—sharp and knowing—and it made him think of his mother. "You look like a million," he said to her.

She poked a playful finger at him. "I'm only eighty-two. Don't push it."

Frank could hear Colleen in the kitchen with his father, helping him put the groceries away. "You didn't have to buy all this food," she was saying.

"We have to eat, don't we?" Pap answered, then complained good-naturedly, "And you cleaned up in here. Why did you do that? Now I won't know where anything is."

Frank called to him, "We're going to give this whole house a cleaning before we leave."

"What's wrong with this house? There's nothing wrong with it."

Greg leapt to his grandfather's defense. "That's what I keep telling them."

"I'm not surprised you'd think so," Frank jabbed at Greg. "You inherited a natural instinct for clutter from your grandfather. But instead of old televisions, you've got old computers."

Greg shook his head. "And you're a perfectionist. Where did you inherit that from?"

"He didn't get it from me," Pap said as he came back into the room. He stood, slightly hunched, and rubbed his hand thoughtfully across his stubbled chin. "Though I had an Uncle John who was like that. 'A place for everything, and everything in its place,' that's what he always said. I don't think there's anything wrong with a little bit of clutter. Just so it's clean clutter."

Colleen joined the fray. "And that's the magic word, Greg. *Clean.* Your three-month-old dirty gym socks don't qualify."

"I wish I had reason to *wear* gym socks," Minnie said. "All I get are orthopedic odor eaters."

Frank eyed his father for signs of change, any proof of what Aunt Minnie had told them in her letter. Pap looked the same as he always did—smiling face, twinkling eyes, thin strands of gray hair adorning his otherwise bald top. Were those brown age spots just above his forehead? Frank couldn't tell. He wore brown polyester trousers and a blue-and-white-checked flannel shirt. *He's starting to dress like an old man,* Frank thought. Had he always, or was Frank only now noticing for the first time? "How are you feeling, Dad?" asked Frank.

"Never felt better."

Frank looked at him surprised. "Really?"

"Well, I *did* feel better one weekend in 1947. Do you remember 1947, Minnie?"

Aunt Minnie was indignant. "You must be joking. I was a mere child."

Pap turned his attention to Vicki. "You're getting awfully big. You better stop growing, or you'll have to marry a basketball player."

Vicki grinned at him. Pap always said that to her. Frank had thought it charming before, but now he wondered if it was another symptom.

"Well, boy, how's school? Last year, right?" Pap asked Greg. Then he suddenly pointed a finger at Greg's goatee. "Are you growing a moustache?"

"Not really," Greg replied, touching his chin self-consciously.

"Did you hear about the man who grew his beard so long that, one day when he was running for the bus, he tripped on it and ran all the way up to his chin?"

Greg laughed politely, but Frank knew that Greg had heard Pap tell that joke dozens of times before.

"Got enough money?" Pap asked and reached for his wallet.

"Don't, Dad. We're fine."

"That's not what I hear. I hear you got laid off. Isn't that right? Though it might've been nice if you'd told me yourself."

Frank shot a disapproving look to Aunt Minnie. She shrugged.

"How many years were you with that company?" Pap asked.

"Twenty."

Pap shook his head. "Nope, that's no good at all."

"It's good to have a career change at my age. I thought I might get on as the window wiper at the car wash." Frank tried to speak lightly, but it sounded hard and dull.

"It'll wrinkle your fingers," Pap retorted. "And how're you gonna afford to keep Greg in school?"

"Or buy me a belly-button ring?" Vicki interjected.

Pap started to fish through his wallet again. "Take some money."

"Put it away. You think *you're* going to pay his tuition with what you've got in there? A dollar and some old business cards won't do it, Dad."

Pap frowned at him. "You can't stop me from giving my grand-children *something*. How about money for Greg's first date with one of those coeds? I've been watching college football games. They're mighty cute."

"That's just TV," said Greg. "All the girls I've seen have thick glasses, crooked teeth, and stringy hair."

"You must be hanging around the English department."

"Watch it, buster. *I* was an English major," Aunt Minnie said.

"My point exactly," Pap said. "You make sure to date while you're in college. That's how I met your grandmother. She was working in the library at the University and I was. . ."

Frank rolled his eyes. "Here we go again." It was a story they'd all heard a million times and could repeat by heart.

This time, though, Pap stopped himself and looked confused. "I was doing something. What was I doing? Help me, Minnie. She was *your* sister."

"How should I know? It was *your* first meeting," she replied.

"You were sisters. I thought you talked about those sorts of things."

"We only talked about the good-looking boys."

"Get out of my house, you old bug."

Aunt Minnie sat down in Pap's favorite easy chair. "The only thing she said about you was that you kept annoying her at the library."

"I kept making noise to get her attention."

"You almost got her fired."

"A small sacrifice for love."

"Maybe for you."

"You were just jealous because I didn't ask *you* out."

Aunt Minnie chuckled and shook her head. By now Greg and Vicki were sitting on the couch like spectators. They watched Pap and Minnie like they watched their favorite television shows.

Pap gestured with great flourish. "I stood on the library steps and sang her a song when she came out. It was a regular serenade on my ukulele. I'll never forget it."

"Neither will we. You bring it up every time we're together," Frank grumbled.

"And then I..." Pap stopped again, a shadow crossing his face. He clearly couldn't remember what happened next. He didn't know what to say. It was an awkward moment, and Frank looked to Aunt Minnie to help.

"The point your grandfather is trying to make," she said to Greg, to recover the situation, "is that you should get yourself to college and meet a woman like your grandmother."

Pap nodded. "That's right. You don't need an education when you have a woman like that. And if you can't find one like her, then look for one like your Aunt Minnie here. In the English department."

"That's *if* I go to college," Greg said with affected nonchalance.

"Now, Greg—" Frank began, but Colleen stepped in like a referee. She spoke quickly. "I think that's enough reminiscing for now."

"Do you have a dog?" Vicki suddenly asked Pap.

"A dog? No, why?"

Colleen deftly fielded the question. "Because we were thinking of getting you one for your birthday. Which reminds me: happy birthday!" She hugged him and kissed him on the cheek.

"Is it my birthday? I forgot," Pap said. "Guess it's 'cause there were no presents around to remind me."

Colleen patted him on the arm. "Be patient."

"Did you all eat? Are you hungry? I made some stew," said Pap, with a brisk rubbing of his hands.

"We had a big breakfast," Frank told him.

Pap looked at his watch. "But it's 2:15. You must be starving."

"It's ten 'til twelve," Greg said.

"Don't argue with me. It'll only take a minute to warm up." Pap hustled off to the kitchen.

"Even less if you use that watch," Greg declared after him.

"His watch has been stopped at 2:15 for three weeks," Minnie informed them quietly.

Vicki leaned to her mother and said, "I hope he isn't going to make the stew out of that dog food."

Gesturing to Aunt Minnie, Frank headed for the front porch. Colleen followed. A moment later, Aunt Minnie stepped out to join them. Though the sun was out, it was cool and Frank shoved his hands into his pockets. The women hugged themselves.

"Well?" Aunt Minnie asked.

"He *looks* good," Colleen said, pleased. "The way you talked on the phone, I expected—"

Minnie held up a hand and double-checked to make sure Pap was still in the kitchen. "We went to the doctor's this morning. That's why we were late."

"Dr. Janssen?"

"No. This was a specialist Dr. Janssen wanted Pap to see. Over in Brownsville." Aunt Minnie looked out towards the street and for a moment Frank saw the age in her face. "It was all I could do to get him there. Finally I had to tell him we were going so that *I* could get a checkup."

"So what happened?" Frank asked.

"He confirmed what Dr. Janssen said. Your father has Alzheimer's disease. And it's getting worse all the time."

"How is it getting worse? Your letter didn't have a lot of details except that he fell down the stairs and keeps losing things."

"It's nothing big, Frank. It's just . . . a lot of little things like I told you on the phone."

"What 'little things'?" Frank asked, checking his volume. "I didn't think falling down the stairs was a 'little thing.' What other kinds of little things are there? Did he get hit by a truck? Maybe he fell asleep underneath a moving bulldozer?"

"Relax, Frank," Colleen said.

Aunt Minnie sighed. She didn't seem to know where to begin. "Did you notice his shoes?"

"His shoes."

"He was wearing slip-ons," Colleen remembered.

Frank looked surprised. His father hated slip-ons. He called them "sissy-shoes." Frank had bought him a pair for Christmas one year, and as far as he knew Pap had never worn them. He searched Minnie's face for answers.

Minnie swallowed hard and said in a soft voice that trembled ever so slightly, "One afternoon a couple of weeks ago I came over, and he was sitting here. Just sitting. He looked like he'd been crying. At first I thought he'd been thinking about Martha . . . he's been doing that a lot lately. Reminiscing a lot about your mother. I guess that's one of the things that happens. With Alzheimer's, I mean. People get more emotional than they used to be. But he *wasn't* crying about your mother. Not this time, at least. He was crying because he'd forgotten how to tie his shoes."

Frank was stunned. Colleen lowered her head.

Minnie wiped her nose with a tissue she'd retrieved from a pocket. "One morning in August, Bill McKendricks found your dad out front in his bathrobe trying to shovel snow off the driveway. Needless to say, it caused quite a stir around here."

"Oh, great." Frank shook his head and paced around the porch.

"I caught him one morning as he was heading out the door for work," Minnie went on.

"Work?"

"He was wearing a pair of overalls and his old miner's cap. He was headed for the mines."

Colleen sat down on the glider. It made rusty noises at her.

Frank scrubbed his chin as he tried to sort through what Minnie was saying. "But is that enough to have him put in a home?" he eventually asked. "Why does he need care?"

Minnie leveled her gaze at Frank. "Apart from doing something dangerous, or hurting himself, he's also having accidents."

"Accidents?" Frank asked.

"You mean *accidents*," Colleen said.

Minnie nodded. "He's losing control of his body."

Frank leaned against the porch rail. *My father is in diapers*, he thought.

"His forgetfulness is chronic," Minnie said. "One evening I came around to find he hadn't eaten all day. He insisted he had, but I could tell he hadn't. When I tried to fix him something, he kept protesting that he'd eaten just a few minutes ago, and I knew full well that he was wrong. Then after I'd fed him and cleared the plates away, he wanted to know when it was time to eat because he was starving."

"This must be awful for you," Colleen said softly. "You should have told us sooner."

"I didn't know what to say," Aunt Minnie replied, tears coming to her eyes. "Everything was spread out over time, so I didn't think it was anything but forgetfulness and confusion. The kind we all get at this age. But now I feel terrible because I can't take care of him. Not the way he needs. And there're the other feelings I get. Feelings I'm ashamed of."

"What kind of feelings?"

"Hurt, mostly. He accused me of stealing his pen. It wasn't even a special pen, just something he'd picked up at the bank. But he couldn't find it, and he called me in a rage. He said I was a thief. I told him I didn't have his pen, that he'd probably misplaced it, but then he called me a liar and hung up. I almost stopped speaking to him altogether for that. But then it dawned on me what was happening. That's when I insisted he go to Dr. Janssen." She sniffled and blew her nose.

Vicki appeared at the screen door, her face a mosaic through the mesh. "You better come in."

There was a loud rumbling coming from the kitchen. When Frank walked in, he saw Pap standing at the sink. The cupboard doors beneath it were open, and Pap was kicking at the pipes. Greg was sitting on a chair rubbing his foot. He gave Frank a helpless look.

"What in the world—," Frank began to say.

"It's all right," Pap said as he continued to jab his foot into the cupboard. "It's the pipes under the sink. They vibrate and make a racket, and you have to kick them."

"I tried," Greg said, still rubbing his foot.

"You've gotta do it a certain way," Pap admonished him. He gave the sink one last kick, and the pipes went quiet. He turned to Greg. "Are you gonna be all right?"

Greg wiggled his foot around. "I think it'll live."

"You should get those pipes fixed, Dad."

"I'm used to them." He waved everyone to the kitchen table. "Everybody sit down, eat some stew."

Aunt Minnie looked at the clock above the sink. "I can't stay. I've got to run."

"Why? What's the rush?" He looked at his watch. "It's only 2:15."

"I'm getting you a new watch, Dad."

"I don't need a new watch, this one works fine. Why are you running off, Minnie?"

"Rose Benson asked me to drive her to the hairdresser's."

"The hairdresser! Again?" Pap protested. "I swear, she's got it a different color every time I see her. I'm gonna start calling her 'Technicolor.'"

Minnie picked up her coat and put it on. "Well, she isn't Technicolor now. She's simply black-and-white. She got caught in one of those automatic sprinkler systems at her son's house, and it rinsed all the color out."

Pap grunted. "I don't know why women fuss with their hair so much. They should leave the color alone. Leave it natural, the way God intended. Who cares if it gets gray? I don't. The whitened hair of the elderly is a crown, isn't that what the Bible says?"

"I don't know," Minnie replied. "I wasn't there when it was written."

"Well, if it doesn't, it *should* say that," Pap insisted. "I'm not ashamed of being old. Seventy-five years is something to be proud of. Don't you think?"

Everyone mumbled their agreements. Frank watched his father curiously. Something was happening that he hadn't seen in years.

Pap's voice got darker and angrier as his face turned red. "You tell those people at the church I said that, too. There's nothing wrong with being old. Tell me I'm too old to teach my class. Tell me I can't do it anymore. I *can* do it. I've been a good Sunday school teacher. Over fifty years at that church, teaching those kids, and now they say I can't—" Pap suddenly stopped himself. He looked at each one of them. "What are you gawking at?" He poked a threatening finger at Greg. "Eat your stew!"

"Sorry, Pap." Greg turned to the table and started to dish out the stew. Vicki, her eyes never leaving her grandfather, also sat down and pulled a bowl towards her.

"What's all this?" Frank asked Minnie quietly.

Minnie shook her head. "The elders at the church asked him to quit teaching his Sunday school class. It's . . . he hasn't . . ."

"Don't talk about me like I'm not here," Pap said.

Minnie walked over to Pap and touched his arm gently. "Don't worry about it, Walter. You've been a good teacher. Bob Simpson said he became a preacher because of your teaching, and he's somewhere in Africa as a missionary. And who knows who else has . . ."

She seemed lost for words. "None of us will know the kind of influence you've had until we gather in heaven, but . . . well, don't worry about it. The folks at the church don't mean anything by it."

Pap stood pouting with his arms folded across his chest. "So I lose my place and ramble a bit. Younger folks do it and no one thinks anything of it." He lapsed into a brooding silence.

Aunt Minnie looked at Frank and Colleen with a sympathetic expression, and then she leaned over Greg and whispered, "It's not him. Just forget about it."

Greg nodded. Minnie gave Pap a quick kiss on the cheek and walked out.

They all sat down to a silence thicker than Pap's stew.

Frank was relieved that it didn't taste like dog food.

∞

PAP DIDN'T EAT. HE said he was tired and went up to his room.

The Reynolds family ate their stew, though no one was hungry. Frank took only a few bites and then decided to go up to talk to Pap.

"Please don't talk to him about moving out," Colleen asked him before he left. "Wait until after the party."

"We'll see," Frank said.

The door was open and Frank could see Pap lying on his bed. He wasn't sleeping. He was reading a Zane Grey paperback, just as he often did. Frank could have been fifteen again and the scene would have been the same. There was his mother sitting across the room at her vanity, brushing her long brown hair, the pots and jars spread out before her. Then she stood at the wardrobe, choosing a dress. She was over at the tallboy, putting laundry away. She smiled at Frank. He blinked, and she was gone. But the room was the same. His father hadn't changed anything in it since her death.

"Dad?"

Pap put down the paperback and looked up at his son. Frank wondered if he'd been crying. With audible effort, Pap sat up. He tried to flatten the crumpled bedsheets and said, "Nobody understands. Nobody could possibly understand."

"I understand, Dad."

"No, you don't."

Frank sat on the edge of the bed. But he didn't know what to say.

Pap's voice was filled with confusion. "I don't know why I got so upset."

"Dad, you've got to tell me what's happening to you."

"Nothing's happening," he said, instantly defensive again. "Things . . . it feels like they're ganging up on me."

"We need to talk. Are you up for talking?" Frank asked.

Pap seemed lost in his own thoughts. "I forget things. Little things that I've known all my life. It's so . . . frustrating. I forget words. I have some days when I can't put my thoughts together. The other day I was talking to Dale Johnson across the street, and I wanted to tell him about the petunias growing in the backyard. But I couldn't think of the word. That word."

"Petunias? A lot of people would forget what they're called."

"I forgot the word 'yard.' I stood there stumbling and stammering like a fool."

Frank patted his father's leg. "Yard is an easy word to forget, Dad. I forget it all the time. It hasn't been mowed in months."

"Don't patronize me," Pap said and rubbed his eyes. "I know why you're here. And don't say it's for my birthday. Minnie told you we went to the doctor. That woman is incapable of keeping a secret."

"Why are you keeping secrets, Dad?"

"The same reason you do. Why didn't you tell me you lost your job?"

"We're talking about you right now."

"I don't want to talk about me." He started digging in his pocket for his wallet again. "You need money, don't you? How much do you need?"

"Nothing, Dad."

"It's a dirty trick laying a man off after he's been there so many years. You're a good worker, Frank. I know it. You were always the conscientious one. Responsible. Everything was neat and orderly for you. And I've been proud of you, Son. Good wife. Fine grandchildren. I've been proud."

Pap looked at Frank anxiously, his voice pleading. "You see? I'm talking fine. I'm not forgetting any of the words. I'm not angry anymore, either. I'll quit teaching my class if that's what they want me to do. They know what's best." He held out his wallet again. "How much do you need?"

Frank suddenly realized that his father was ducking and dodging, throwing out a smoke screen of words to keep him at bay. "I don't want to talk about money. I want to talk about you."

"There's nothing to talk about," Pap said. "Minnie shouldn't have told you anything. The doctors are confused."

"Are they?"

Pap pressed his lips together. They went thin and white.

"Dad?"

Then he blurted it out. "She wants me to move. Can you believe it? She thinks I should move out of this house."

"She's worried," Frank explained. "We all are. We think you should get into a place where you can be cared for."

"I can't sell this house. It's *my* house. I'm fine, Frank. I just have moments. Everyone has moments."

"Dad—"

"I'm seventy-five years old. I'm just showing some signs of my age. Let's see how *you* are when you're seventy-five."

"I hope you're around for that," said Frank. He shifted his position and tried to sound reasonable, practical. "Look, you can't stay here alone—"

Pap shook his head defiantly. "It's in my will, Frank. You'll get it when I die. But not before. I won't sell the house. I won't move out. I'm not sick."

"You're not?" Frank challenged him. "Look at your shoes, Dad. Why are you wearing shoes without laces?"

Pap shrugged. "It's the latest style. I read it in *People* magazine."

"Shoveling snow in the middle of August—is that the latest style, too?"

"I'll have to look in *People.*"

Frank frowned at him.

"I wasn't feeling well. I was sleepwalking. You used to sleepwalk, too, and I didn't ask you to sell your house and move out."

"Come on, Dad. What'll it be next—playing jacks in the middle of Route 40? Or maybe you'll go wandering off completely. I'll have to put your picture on shopping bags and milk cartons. Be reasonable."

Pap folded his arms. "I'm being reasonable. *You're* not being reasonable."

Frank knew it was a losing battle. "We won't talk about this now."

"We won't talk about this *ever*," Pap said, his voice shaking. "I've been in this house for a long time. All that I am is in this house, and you want me to walk away from it. Where will I go? You're not thinking about keeping me here. You want me to go away from Peabody. Take my house, take my town, and I'll have nothing left."

Frank stood up. "Never mind, Dad."

Pap wagged a finger at him. "You left because you wanted to. You always hated this town, and I don't know why. You've been trying to get me to leave here for years. Ever since your mother died. I don't want to. I like this town."

"It's dying."

"We all are," Pap stated. "That's no reason to panic and sell the house and leave town. It's my *home*, Frank. I won't do it. End of discussion."

"All right, Dad. Calm down."

"I *am* calm."

"I said forget about it." Frank walked out of the room, upset that their conversation had gone so wrong. He'd known Pap wouldn't agree easily or go quietly, but he'd harbored the hope that Pap might surprise him.

Halfway down the stairs he heard his father behind him. Pap said lightly, "You wanna play checkers? We haven't played checkers in a long time."

"I don't want to play checkers. You cheat."

Pap sounded affronted. "How can I cheat at checkers?"

"You always tip the board over when you know you've lost."

He chuckled. "That used to make you furious."

"It still does." At the bottom of the stairs, Frank turned towards the front door.

"Get the board, Son," Pap said.

Frank grabbed his coat. "I want to take a walk. Maybe I'll go downtown and count funeral processions. Greg'll play."

Pap held onto the banister as if to steady himself. He said quietly. "You don't like me much, do you?"

Frank gazed at him without answering, his mind full of all the things he wished he could say.

"That's okay, you know," Pap said. "You can love someone but not like them sometimes."

"That's a good thing, Dad," Frank said.

⚇

FRANK WALKED DOWN BRADDOCK Street, past the wood and stone houses and square lawns, the elderly trees with their changing leaves, and the memories of people long gone who called to him from their porch swings. *I wish these ghosts would leave me alone,* Frank thought. He walked past the Sizemore house and, of course, the memory of Kathy Sizemore sprang to mind. She'd been his first real love. And as if no time had passed, he could see her in the driveway, waving to him, her smile as radiant as he remembered, her hair a golden glow and her slender body made all the more attractive by a baggy University sweatshirt and cutoff jeans. She stood with a hose in one hand, a sponge in the other, her white Mustang gleaming wet behind her.

Frank blinked and the memory vanished, replaced by the reality of an empty, cracked driveway and chipped white garage door that needed a new coat of paint. He wondered where Kathy was now. What was she doing? Was she happily married? Did she have children? Did she ever wonder about him?

For a fleeting moment he felt that feeling again, the longing that Peabody seemed to stir. Not for Kathy, necessarily. He knew he wouldn't trade his years with Colleen for anyone or anything. But he longed for the innocence of that first love he'd had for Kathy. The tingle he'd felt in his gut when they'd first held hands. The breathlessness that had squeezed his heart when they'd kissed. The ease of their conversations, the joy of their outings, the single-mindedness and naïveté of their companionship.

He remembered one picnic they'd taken together that should have been a true disaster. The sodas had been warm, the sandwiches dry, and the dessert she'd made special for the occasion had got crushed under a sneaker that fell off the back shelf of his car when he'd stopped too fast at a light. But, undaunted, they had turned the little disasters into a joke. Frank laughed harder that day than he'd ever laughed before. Even when it rained on them, and they had to dash into the shelter of the gazebo in the park, it was all right. The rain drummed like fingers on the roof. He could still see her turning towards him, as if in slow motion, her hair flying wet, and her smile so wide that the dimples showed on both sides of her mouth. Her eyes were half-open, blinking away the drops that fell from her forehead. She was so beautiful, almost transcendent. Then she announced, laughing, "What a perfect day!" And they exchanged a look of such purity and joy that Frank knew something had changed in his perception of the world. He seemed to stand outside of time itself.

Frank prayed that God would freeze the moment. He wanted to feel every sensation, relish every impression, as if he'd come alive for the first time in his life—as if in this one moment, all the best moments of life could be contained. Frank was overcome with the suspicion—no, call it a *conviction*—that there would be other moments in life that stood outside of time. Glimpses of something like heaven, or eternity, or whatever you wanted to call it.

But the moment passed and Frank was left with an indescribable ache, a longing, that he treasured and regretted at the same time. Summer ended, and Frank and Kathy went their separate ways to different colleges and whatever the future held for them. But the longing continued. And Peabody brought it back to him more vividly than anywhere else on earth.

Frank shook his head and turned away from the memory of the moment that, like so many others, had faded. What was the point of longing for what he couldn't have? He had to decide what to do about his father. He had to figure out where to find a job. He had to convince Greg to go to college.

Downtown had changed more dramatically than Frank had realized. Boring government offices had taken over many of the small shops. The other spaces were empty, covered with notices and bills. Hayes Department Store, the headquarters of good taste and fashion for so many years, was also vacant except for those weekends advertised on signs in the dingy windows when the main floor was used as a flea market. The marquee on the Coliseum announced: *For Rent*. Frank assumed it wasn't the name of a movie.

Surprisingly, Ben's Barber Shop, with the spinning red-and-white candy cane pole, was still in business. Ben was inside, busily cutting some old codger's hair. Frank paused to look at the faded posters in the front window, advertising Brylcreem and various hair tonics that hadn't been manufactured for a long time now.

Mr. Pierce, the owner of Michelle's Café, with its "gay nineties" style, stood with broom in hand under the long pink awning that stretched out to the curb. He waved and Frank waved back, even though he was certain Mr. Pierce didn't know who he was.

Frank passed a tattoo parlor called "Tattoos While U-Wait." This gave Frank a momentary pause as he wondered whether there was any other way to get a tattoo.

Frank stopped at the Sunshine Florist shop and decided to take flowers to his mother's grave. He hadn't been there in a few years. A woman Frank vaguely remembered—from the Binnocek family, he thought—helped him pick out a colorful bouquet of carnations and daffodils with a sprinkling of angel's breath. He had no idea what was appropriate for a grave, but tried to pick flowers he thought his mother would like.

Bealle's Memorial Park was on the other side of town; it took Frank longer than he'd expected to walk there. The cemetery had originally been beside a church, but the church had burned down sometime in the nineteenth century. Now it was part of the Bealle conglomeration of funeral homes and memorial parks, with iron fences and trim grass and not an errant fallen leaf to be found. The older sections contained gravestones going all the way back to Colonial times. Frank strode straight to his mother's grave, easily found nestled next to a grove of strategically placed trees. He looked at the angled bronze markers—two of them, one with his mother's final particulars and the other with his father's unfinished particulars.

Once the whole family had gone to the grave with his father. Greg had asked Pap very innocently, "Is it strange standing here, looking down at your name on your future grave?"

Without missing a beat, Pap replied, "As long as I'm standing here looking down on the grave, it doesn't bother me at all."

Frank put the flowers on his mother's plot of earth. The ground was soft and moss-like. Since childhood, Frank had always felt that cemetery earth was too squishy, as if you might suddenly sink into one of the graves below. The flowers looked artificially colorful against the brown grass, the bronze marker, and the gray stone. The sun disappeared behind thick clouds.

Lowering his head, Frank began to pray: *Dear Father in heaven...* but any additional words escaped him. What did he want to tell God? What did he want God to do? Fix everything for him, make it all right? Was God even around to witness any of this?

Frank sighed deeply. He had been in one of those Christian bookstores the other day and had seen a whole row of biographies about people who had overcome great physical trauma to glorify God. Maybe it was the latest trend: be a victim, write a book, make a fortune. But losing your job wasn't dramatic. Who cared about that? Growing old wasn't dramatic either. Nobody writes a book about those things. Why should they? Who ever claimed the victory of God because an unemployment form had been filled out correctly? Or who ever wrote a best-selling, faith-affirming book because they'd grown old? How was God glorified in forgetfulness, temper tantrums, institution-green walls, and bedpans?

He stood for a moment, surprised by a feeling of despair that caused him to shiver. No one had told him that losing your job was like losing a loved one. No one had said that grief would come like dry heaves.

Frank left the grave and made his way back through town. He remembered that there was a nursing home housed in what had once been an oil baron's mansion—a monstrous red-stone building that looked like a set from *Dark Shadows* and had spooked him when he was a boy. It wouldn't take him too far out of his way to stop in and get information. He tried to think of what it was called. Something soothing about a garden, he thought.

∞

GREG SAT IN THE big easy chair in the living room, headphones clamped to his head. His favorite music—a compilation of songs he'd downloaded from the Internet before the trip—thumped away in his ears. He gazed at the room and wished he'd brought his laptop computer. He'd left it behind as a concession to his mother. But now he sat by himself, the family scattered for different reasons, and regretted his decision. There wasn't anything for him to do.

He took the headphones off for a moment and listened. In a distant part of the basement, Pap was banging around the coal furnace. It was supposed to be cold that night, and Pap said he wanted the furnace stoked properly. Greg could hear Pap through the vent in the wall, though he didn't know what exactly Pap was doing. He knew the noises, though—such as the squeaky iron door opening. Maybe Pap was shoveling the coal in, or opening and closing flues. He'd grown up with those sounds when he had visited, and they often greeted him early on a cold winter's morning, or at night as they were going to sleep. His father had wanted Pap to get a new and more efficient furnace, but Pap wasn't interested. The coal furnace was like an old friend, Pap had said at the time. "I know it better than I know the back of my hand."

Greg turned on four televisions before he found the one that worked. An old movie, football games, an infomercial for a new kind of mop. . . Pap's cable company was as boring as the one they had at home. He turned the television off and put his headphones back on. The music served as a soundtrack to his thoughts.

Ch-ch-ch-ch-changes, David Bowie sang.

Now that was an ironic song to hear while Greg sat in a room that seemed to defy change. The magazines on the end table could have been pulled from a time capsule of the late sixties and early seventies. There was an old *Guideposts* with Johnny Unitas in uniform on the cover. Billy Graham's *Decision* magazine had a story about a British pop star named Cliff Richard. *Stories From the Wild West* chronicled the career of Wild Bill Hickock. And beneath these were a handful of women's magazines that had already been out-of-date before Greg's grandmother had died.

Greg sank deeper into the chair. He found comfort in this room, in the whole house. It defied the ongoing changes that marked his world—new technologies, new complications, new *everything*. Where he had once noticed change only in seasons, and moves from one school class to another, or one grade to another, or the year his voice broke, now it came from everywhere. He was going to graduate from high school. He had to make decisions about his future. He had to give in to change.

That's why it was reassuring to come to his grandfather's. Change wasn't an issue here. At least it hadn't been until now.

Greg felt a tight fist of anxiety push into his stomach. If Pap had to go into a nursing home, then they'd sell this house, and another thread to the past would be cut. If his dad didn't find a new job, then they might have to sell *their* house and move to a different part of the country.

Greg's mind spun with contradictions. Hadn't he lectured his father about the error of staying in the same job, doing variations on the same thing, for over twenty years? This change would be good for his father, Greg believed. It seemed wrong, somehow, for a man to become so entrenched into a single way of life. Where was the adventure? Where was the *spark*? But wasn't Greg being hypocritical by demanding change from his father but resisting this change for Pap?

Greg tried to shrug off the questions. He didn't have any answers, nor did he expect any. Things simply happened, and you had to roll with them. Or was it really that easy? Wasn't God out there somewhere watching over them—maybe even orchestrating the changes? Or was he watching from the bench, a nonplayer, a mere spectator?

Now Greg wished even more that he had his laptop with him. He wanted to talk to his friends on the Internet. They would understand his feelings. They would have opinions. And that was another irony about his world of change. Though the technology changed relentlessly, the Internet was constant. It didn't matter how things changed in his life, his friends on the Internet would be there. Whether or not Greg moved to another house, city, or country—he could still log on and chat with them as if they were in the same room. His friends on the Internet were blind to change.

"Ahem," Pap cleared his throat. He was standing next to the couch with a wooden checkerboard sitting like a tray in his hands. "You must be trying to solve the problems of the world."

Taking off his headphones Greg looked up at his grandfather, remembering Pap's outburst earlier and the uncharacteristic way he'd lashed out at them. Colleen had assured Greg and Vicki that it wasn't really Pap but rather his illness that had spoken. But it left Greg uneasy, wondering if something like that might happen again. Like right now.

Pap held out the checkerboard. "Let's play."

"Only if you promise not to cheat," Greg replied as playfully as he could.

Pap looked at him indignantly, but there was a twinkle in his eyes. "Don't *you* start."

Greg pulled a rickety old TV dinner stand over from a corner, along with a chair from the kitchen. Pap sat down in his favorite easy chair. They set up the pieces and started to play. Greg welcomed the chance to talk to Pap alone. Actually, he had been wanting to discuss the future and the conflict he knew was coming with his father. Pap might understand. Pap might know what to do. But now...

He gazed at Pap for a moment. His hair was grayer than last time, the wrinkles deeper; there were broken red veins on his cheeks, and a section of facial hair he'd missed with the razor right under his nose. He looked tired, too.

Pap suddenly tapped the table. "Are you going to just sit there and daydream? It's your move."

Greg looked at the board. "Oh, yeah." He quickly moved a piece.

Pap moved a piece and clapped his hands. "Crown me."

Greg stared at the board, unsure of how Pap's piece had suddenly wound up on his end.

"Your dad and I used to play all the time," Pap said while Greg crowned the piece. "He was a very *serious* player. He acted like he was playing chess or something. That's no way to play checkers. Checkers is for fun. Chess is for brain cramps. I hope his walk helps him unwind a little."

"Me, too." But Greg didn't think it would. He suspected the walk would make his father all the more determined. After all, his father had problems to solve.

Pap nodded as if he knew what Greg was thinking. "He's got a lot on his mind. He's on edge. It's the way of the world—a man works for twenty years and what happens? He gets laid off. The same happened to me when I worked at the coal mine. No sooner had I gotten out of the mine and into a supervisor's position than they shut down the mine."

"What did you do?"

"I went to work for the railroad." Pap chuckled. "Now *that* was a growth industry. I sure knew how to pick them."

Greg suddenly remembered a scene from long before: His grandfather coming home from his shift at the Peabody station, wearing his chipped black working boots and dark blue uniform. For years Greg had believed Pap was actually an engineer on a train, wearing a red scarf around his neck and tooting the whistle. Only recently did Greg learn that Pap was actually in charge of local freight and never rode on the trains.

"Your father needs to relax and have a little more faith," Pap said. "The Lord'll provide. He always has. It's the only way I've made it. You live this long, and you see some bad times. But even at its worst, God was there. We never went hungry. We always had a roof over our heads. God is good." He suddenly pointed a bony finger at Greg. "Don't you forget it."

"I won't." Greg double-jumped Pap's pieces and landed in a crown square on Pap's side of the board.

Pap looked surprised. "What was that? What do you call that move?"

Greg shrugged. "It was a move. I got your pieces and now I'm waiting to be crowned."

"I don't think you can move like that in checkers."

"Of course I can. It was a double-jump, and I got your pieces."

Pap shook his head.

"Pap, don't start," Greg said. He'd known this was how it would be. This was part of Pap's strategy. Greg didn't really mind, though. When you played with Pap, this was as much a part of the game as the pieces themselves.

"Don't tell me not to start. In all my years of checkers. . ." Pap scratched at his chin and then pointed at the board. "And I just had that one crowned! Jump a man when he gets crowned. That's not very Christian."

"It's in the rules," Greg said.

"Forget the rules. We're not under the rules, we're under grace. Put that piece back on the board!"

"But—"

"Put it back," Pap said firmly.

Greg didn't move, wondering how far he could push Pap. They stared at each other.

"*Put it—*"

Greg gave in and put the crowned piece back onto the board.

Pap smiled. "Good boy."

Greg grumbled, "I know what you're doing."

"Quit talking and move."

"I'm afraid to."

"Go on. Don't be a sissy."

Greg carefully moved his piece. "Nothing wrong with *that* move, I hope."

Pap scrutinized the board. "Nope."

While Pap tried to decide his next move, Greg leaned back in his chair. This seemed like as good a time as any to broach the subject. "I've got a problem, Pap."

"What's her name?"

"It's not a her."

"It isn't? Then you *do* have a problem."

Greg leaned forward again and tugged at a thread that had come loose from the end of his sleeve. "I really don't want to go to college."

"You don't?" Pap looked disappointed. "But what about meeting the coeds?"

"I'll meet them some other time," Greg replied. "Sometime later. Besides, that's no reason to go to college."

"It's more fun than getting an education."

Greg gazed at his grandfather. "You're not helping me."

Pap nodded. "All right."

"I don't know what to do."

"But I thought you wanted a degree. Didn't you say it was the only way to get ahead in this world—what with all the techno-thingies and thingamajigs you like to play with?"

"I never said that. It's *Dad* who wants me to get a degree."

"I see," Pap said thoughtfully. "So, have you told him?"

"I keep trying to, but he won't listen." Greg hesitated. "The thing is, he doesn't think I have a plan. I *have* a plan. I just don't have his ambitions."

"What's your plan?"

"I'm going to hang around, soak up life, and try to figure things out."

"You call that a plan?"

"Sure," Greg replied, trying to keep his defenses up. "It's not a plan the way you or Dad think of plans. But that's the difference between our generations. We don't think *conventionally* the way you do." Greg paused. "No offense."

"None taken."

"I've seen where nine-to-five at the office leads. There's a better way of doing it."

"Like what?"

"That's what I want to figure out."

Pap didn't say anything for a moment, then he shrugged. "I'm the wrong person to ask right now. There's a rumor going around that I'm not of sound mind. But maybe you're right. Maybe my generation has it all wrong. You live and you work and you raise a family and it all ends with . . . with *what?*"

Greg didn't have an answer.

Suddenly, Pap said, "The future is what you make of it, Greg. If going to college will give you the tools to make it something good and worthwhile, then go to college. If it won't, then skip it. You're a smart kid. You'll do the right thing."

They resumed the game, and Greg wondered if that was it—if that was as much as he would hear from Pap on the subject.

Pap moved his piece. "You get used to it, you know."

"Used to what?"

"The idea of death."

Greg became confused. Had they been talking about death?

Pap slowly touched one of the pieces. "You get to this age, and you have to make peace with it. Make peace or go crazy. And you learn not to make any long-term plans."

Greg decided to roll with the conversation. "Like what?" he asked.

"Minnie won't buy green bananas anymore."

"She won't?"

"She doesn't know if she'll be around when they ripen," Pap said as he grabbed a piece and heartily double-jumped his way towards Greg. "Ha! Take that! Double jump!" He smiled with self-satisfaction as he claimed his victims. "And you thought you could take advantage of an old man. I know your ruse, using that conversation about college to distract me."

"But, Pap—"

"It's no good trying to haggle your way out of it."

"Pap—"

"Forget it, Greg. The victory is mine."

"But you just double-jumped your own pieces."

Pap looked down at the board, his face frozen in a half smile, his brow knitted above the center of his nose.

"We don't have to play anymore," Greg offered.

"I did that on purpose," Pap bluffed. "It was . . . to protect my pieces. You can take them off of the board and save them for when you really need them."

Greg folded his arms. "I've never heard of that."

"It's the way I've always played. Over seventy years. Always."

Greg was unconvinced. "You taught me how to play, and I've never heard of that rule. Put those pieces back."

"It's. . ." Pap paused. Greg could almost hear the wheels turning in Pap's mind. "It's an upper-level rule."

"It is not. Put them back."

"It's for expert players."

"Pap—"

It was another showdown, and this time it was Pap who gave in. He put his pieces back onto the board. Scowling, he said, "I thought you were ready for the upper-level games but apparently you're not. You want to be an amateur all your life."

"Pap—"

"Be quiet and move!" Pap barked.

Unsure whether Pap was serious or not, Greg moved a piece.

"Don't be silly," Pap said softly.

Greg looked over at Pap. "What do you mean?"

Pap scrutinized the checkerboard, his cheeks suddenly going crimson. "Now, wait a minute. Let me think."

Greg was worried now. "Pap?"

Pap stared at the board longer, then said abruptly, "I don't want to play anymore."

"What?" Greg asked, alarmed. Had he hurt Pap's feelings? "You can put your pieces back on if it means that much to you."

Pap shook his head.

"Then what's wrong?" asked Greg.

Pap looked up at Greg with a pained expression on his face. "I can't remember. Am I black or red?"

∞∞

PAP SETTLED DOWN IN front of the television while Greg packed up the checkerboard and checkers and put away the small table. While he did, Colleen and Vicki walked in with packages and a large cake box. A breath of cold air chased them in.

Greg noticed that his mother was red-faced. "I didn't expect to take so long," she puffed. "What time is it?"

Pap looked at his watch. "Two—"

"Never mind. It must be after three at least." Colleen took the cake box out to the kitchen but called back, "We would've been home sooner but Thelma at the bakery had to tell me all the latest gossip."

"She talked about everybody who died," Vicki added unhappily.

"She's a walking obituary column," Pap said. "Nobody kicks the bucket around here without telling her first."

Vicki rolled her eyes. "She couldn't remember what kind of frosting we wanted."

"But she remembered down to the button what clothes everyone was buried in," Colleen added.

"Thelma's a couple of cookies short of a dozen, if you know what I mean," Pap said. "Too many years sniffing vanilla extract."

"Where's Frank?" Colleen asked.

"He said he wants me to sell the house so I shot him," Pap replied. "He's buried in the basement."

"Oh. Then I shouldn't have bought such a large cake," Colleen said as she went back into the kitchen. Soon cupboard doors were opening and closing, and the final preparations for the evening party were under way.

A classic Colleen Reynolds move, Greg observed. Somehow—and Greg didn't know how—she had the ability to take any potentially awkward or tense situation and defuse it. She had been that way Greg's entire life. Battles with teachers, conflicts with neighbors, a falling out with a friend, his mother navigated those unpredictable waters with ease and grace. His dad had once said that she was like a duck: On the surface, she appeared calm, but beneath the surface her legs were paddling wildly.

It bothered Greg. He believed there were times when only a face-to-face, knock-down-drag-out could resolve a problem. Confront it, get it all out honestly and candidly, and then an answer would present itself. But his mother's smooth diversions, her uncanny instincts, deftly avoided the conflict.

A few minutes later, Colleen reappeared from the kitchen and announced that it would be a good idea to go up to the attic and look for some costumes for the party.

"Costumes?" Pap asked.

"It's a costume party," Colleen explained. "Didn't Minnie tell you?"

"No," Pap said with a snort. "And she knows better than to think I'm going to dress up in a silly costume."

"I thought you loved costume parties," Vicki said. "Don't you remember the Fourth of July, the one before Grandma died? You dressed up as Paul Revere."

"Maybe I did then, but now I'd look like a fool."

Colleen was undaunted. "Come on, it'll be fun. I'm sure the attic is full of great things."

"The moths digested those clothes years ago."

Colleen went to him and tugged at his arm. "No birthday presents for you if you don't."

Groaning, Pap dragged himself to his feet. "All right, but I'm not going alone. The monsters'll get me."

The four of them ascended the stairs to the attic. Years ago Pap and Grandma had turned it from a dusty old storage area into a large dormitory-type bedroom for their various grandkids and relatives to stay in. Though the floorboards creaked loudly and the once-fashionable wallpaper had yellowed, Greg was still enchanted by the room. The four beds that lined the wall had been the setting of a lot of kids' play among the cousins, especially after the adults had told them "for the last time" to go to sleep. Greg had already staked his claim here—his things were thrown onto one of the beds.

"Oh," Colleen exclaimed, wrinkling her nose and opening the two dormer windows to let some fresh air in. "It smells terribly musty."

"I don't come up here much," Pap said.

A couple of old wardrobes sat on opposite walls. Colleen and Vicki attacked them first. Pap opened a door that led to the spaces over the eaves. He reached in and yanked the chain to the single bulb that hung just inside.

Greg followed him. This door—and all the junk that had collected behind it—had always been a point of fascination for Greg as he was growing up. There was an old pedal-powered sewing machine, some broken chairs, the shell of a console record player, and a small electric organ with most of its keys missing. A box of old 78s had tipped over, the black vinyl looking like pools of oil. Greg glanced at the artists, some he'd heard of, some he hadn't. Tommy Dorsey, Jimmy Dorsey, Bing Crosby, the Mills Brothers, and Glenn Miller all listed on labels of silver, burgundy, white, and black.

Old toys that had been given to Uncle Dennis and Dad for their birthdays or Christmases long gone also gathered there. Most of them were broken, but that didn't stop Greg from examining them. The remains of a large plastic pinball game leaned against the wall, one of its three legs missing. A child's version of an adult workbench rested among thick cobwebs. Greg knew it had been his father's—even now the wooden tools were still in their proper places. Railroad tracks littered the floor, while the train cars themselves lay like corpses nearby. Years before, the running of the trains around the Christmas tree had been a beloved family tradition. Pap would spend hours setting it up, and then with great fanfare one lucky grandchild would throw the power switch. That was the second thing that announced the arrival of Christmas. The first, of course, was the arrival of the Sears Christmas Wish Book.

There was a small battery-operated shooting gallery with cardboard ducks that quacked their way from one end to the other. The goal was to hit as many as you could with the small plastic balls that shot from a toy rifle. Greg remembered hearing that Uncle Dennis often shot Frank—and once got him solidly in the eye with one. He had to be rushed to the emergency room.

Old trunks sat like small islands in the sea of debris. Pap moved from one to another, throwing open the lids to check the contents. "Let's try this one," he said, then motioned to Greg to help him carry it out. They sat it in the center of the floor, and Pap fiddled with the front lock until it clicked and the lid opened.

Colleen and Vicki descended upon the trunk, jabbering as they pulled the clothes out. Vicki marveled over her grandmother's wedding dress, now a pale yellow with dirty stitching. Colleen looked at Pap's railroad uniform and a few token citations and medals from his days in the military. Greg admired a dark suit with wide lapels and cuffs on the trouser legs—and the black-and-white shoes that came with it.

They pressed the clothes to themselves, or made Greg serve as a model—much to Greg's chagrin. He didn't mind putting on an old uniform or shirt, but he drew the line at a corset, skirt, and bonnet.

Pap watched, a childlike expression on his face. "I'd forgotten about most of this stuff. Look at this." He grabbed an old fedora and dropped it on his head. "What a classic. Clark Gable, huh?"

"More like Jerry Lewis on a bad day," Greg said.

Colleen pulled out a tall trophy with a silver dart on the top. "You should have this out on display."

"Good idea," Frank said from the top of the attic stairs. "People can impale themselves on it as they walk past it."

"Oh, Frank, just in time. We're looking for costumes for the party," Colleen said.

Frank grunted and moved into the room. Greg knew his father's moods well enough to recognize that the walk hadn't helped anything. He looked tired.

Pap held the trophy and gazed at it fondly. "The Interfaith Dart League—1963. We beat the Brownfield Synagogue in the play-offs. I guess that showed 'em who *really* knows God."

"Here's a Sunday school certificate," Colleen announced, holding up an old frame. "You got it for perfect attendance in fourth grade."

"Mrs. Skelton. What a wonderful teacher she was. Led me to Christ." Pap paused for a moment. "It broke her heart when she had to stop teaching."

Frank flipped through a small black book. "I want to know who Judith McKenzie was. You have two stars next to her name."

"What is that?"

"An address book."

Pap grabbed for it. "Give me that."

Frank held the book away. "Not until you tell me who these people are."

"People I knew *before* I got married. Most of them are dead now."

"Did you put the stars in before or after they died?" Vicki asked.

"It's a date book," Frank explained to her as he thumbed through the pages. "You have three stars next to someone named Anastasia. And Kathy Fitzgibbons got *four* stars."

"Pap, please don't tell me you were rating those girls," Colleen said.

Pap hung his head in an insincere show of shame.

"Men!" Colleen snorted.

Pap leaned to Greg and said in a conspiratorial tone: "Kathy was a knockout back then."

"What about now?"

Shaking his head, Pap said, "I saw her at the grocery store the other day. She's had so many face-lifts that her nose is in the middle of her forehead."

"Stop, Pap," Colleen protested.

"She sneezed and nearly blew her eyelashes off."

"I see you've got *five* stars next to Martha Lyons," Frank said.

"Who was that?" asked Greg.

"Your grandmother."

Greg blushed. "Oh." He had forgotten her last name.

Colleen held up a yellowed piece of paper. "Here's your wedding certificate. There's a photo taped to it, too."

Greg and Vicki gathered around to look at the cracked black-and-white photo. Pap stood on the steps of a church, a tall and striking young man in a dark suit, his hands at his side. Grandma stood next to him wearing a plain dress and a bridal veil. They looked uncomfortable, as if having their picture taken was the worst part of the day—which Greg imagined it was.

They handed the photo to Pap, who looked at it for a long time. He made a noise that sounded like a cough (or a stifled sob, Greg thought) then suddenly stood up. "I'm going to put on some coffee."

Colleen waved a hand to stop him. "I'll do it."

He shooed her away. "Thanks anyway."

When Colleen was sure Pap was out of earshot, she said, "Maybe this wasn't such a good idea."

"We can't walk on eggshells all the time," Frank said. He pulled some folded papers from his back pocket. "At least that's what they said at The Faded Flower."

"The Faded Flower?"

Frank explained that The Faded Flower Retirement Community was housed in the old Grayson Mansion and had sections dedicated to old people with all kinds of needs. Everything from moderate care to full service, the copy said. "It may be the place to put him," Frank concluded.

"Do we have to talk about this now?" Colleen asked.

Frank shrugged. "If not now, when?"

Greg picked up an old leather-backed book. It was a King James version of the Bible. He flipped open the cover and read in a distinctive pen-and-ink cursive: "For Walter, from Mother and Father—1936." The pages were coming away from the seam and some of the verses had been marked with a blue pen.

"We've been here all day, and there've been no serious problems," Colleen told Frank.

"He still cheats at checkers," Greg said as he carefully looked through the Bible. John chapter three, verse sixteen, leapt out at him. "For God so loved the world, that he gave his only begotten Son, that whosoever believeth in him should not perish, but have everlasting life." From elsewhere in the house, Greg could hear the sound of the pipes rumbling—then silence. Pap must have given them a good kick.

"Maybe it's too soon to talk about moving him," Colleen said.

Frank shook his head. "What about his outburst this morning?"

"We all have outbursts," Colleen argued. "You've had a few yourself."

"You can say that again," Vicki said under her breath. Greg offered her a sympathetic look.

Frank glared at Vicki and shoved the flyer back into his pocket. He turned to Colleen again and said, "Minnie knows more about it than we do, and she thinks he needs someone to watch over him. Besides, the director of The Faded Flower said that Pap could go into one of the low-maintenance wings. It'd be like living in his own apartment. He'd hardly notice that anyone was keeping an eye on him."

Colleen sighed. "It doesn't seem right somehow."

They could hear Pap coming back up the stairs, so they returned to looking through what was left in the trunk. Pap seemed to notice the silence. Then he noticed the book in Greg's lap. "My old Bible."

"I was looking at some of the verses you marked," Greg said.

"My parents marked them," Pap explained. "They made me memorize those verses."

"Do you still remember them?"

"Try me."

Greg randomly flipped to one of the pages in the back. "James chapter one, verses two and three."

"'My brethren, count it all joy when ye fall into divers temptations; knowing this, that the trying of your faith worketh patience.'" Pap looked directly at Frank. "Not bad for a senile old man who can't take care of himself . . . and still has very good hearing." He gave Frank a toothy smile.

Frank tipped his head to Greg. "Take a look at Titus chapter two—" But before Greg could find it, Frank recited: "'Aged men be sober, grave, temperate, sound in faith, in charity, in patience.'"

"Yep, that's a good one," Pap said. "But I like Ephesians six where it says to 'Obey your parents in the Lord: for this is right. Honour thy father and mother . . . that it may be well with thee, and thou mayest live long on the earth.'"

"The rest of that is pretty good, too," Frank countered. "'And, ye fathers, provoke not your children to wrath.'"

"I also like . . ." Pap began, but he obviously couldn't think of another verse. He grabbed the Bible from Greg. "Give me that book."

"What're you going to do, hit him with it?" Greg asked. He was starting to feel anxious again. This game of dueling Bible verses had an awful edge to it.

Colleen interceded, "I think that's enough Bible-bashing for now. Aunt Minnie will be here soon. No bloodshed before the party."

Pap pouted like a small child, and at first Greg thought it was a joke. "No respect. No respect at all." Pap spun towards the stairs angrily.

"Dad, wait," Frank said.

Pap held up a hand. "No. I'm going to make some coffee."

"You're making *more* coffee?" Colleen asked.

"Why? Did you already make some?" Pap asked her.

Colleen looked confused. "No," she said. *"You* did."

"No, I didn't," Pap said.

"Then what did you just do in the kitchen?" Frank asked.

"When?"

"Just now."

"I wasn't in the kitchen. I've been standing here talking to you." He looked impatiently at Frank. "Quit joking around. You're making me nervous."

"I'm not joking," Frank said.

"Stop it!" Pap suddenly shouted. "You're trying to make me think I need help. I don't! Do you hear me? I'm going to make coffee. For the *first* time." He stormed down the stairs.

Frank and Colleen looked at each other. Greg found himself chewing at his lower lip.

"I hope everyone wants a lot of coffee," said Vicki.

∞

GREG WANTED TO MAKE himself scarce until it was time for the party, so he hid in the attic and paced from one end of the room to the other. He tried to ease his sense of worry about his grandfather. He'd never seen Pap so volatile—the way he exploded about the church, his anger and confusion about the coffee. It was so unlike him and Greg, who had hoped his father had been exaggerating about Pap's condition, now had to concede that things really were bad.

This weekend was a huge mistake and this party will end in disaster, Greg thought as he paced. *Maybe I can hide up here until it's all over.*

No such luck. Colleen shouted for him from the bottom of the stairs. She had things for him to do—and she demanded that he dress up in Pap's old suit—the one they'd found earlier with the double-breasted jacket and cuffed pants. Greg reluctantly obeyed and tried it on. The jacket and trousers were much too large, and Greg felt as if he were swimming inside of them. Then he had the wild hope that he could disappear into the clothes completely and not be dragged out for the party.

Colleen dressed up in an old flapper's dress she found in another trunk.

"Pretty racy for an old Free Methodist," Frank observed.

"Your mother wasn't a Free Methodist," Colleen corrected him. "She came from a family of Episcopalians who were downright worldly."

To Greg, the skirt seemed too short and the neckline too low. He was embarrassed to see his mother look so ... so ... *young.*

Vicki bought some fake stick-on tattoos from the pharmacy around the corner and decided to dress as a biker—though she wore her own T-shirt and jeans and looked pretty much as she always did. Every now and then she'd jingle some car keys and mention the Harley she'd parked in the back. Later she found a small square box to roll up in one of her T-shirt sleeves. "It's supposed to be a box of cigarettes," she explained.

Frank, who was in no mood to dress up, finally put on his father's army jacket as a concession. Greg knew the dark clouds were gathering over his father's mood. Pap had been baiting and teasing Frank all afternoon about the house. For the most part, Frank had deflected the comments good-naturedly, but Greg could see that they were wearing on him. Frank was getting impatient and, if pushed too hard, would retaliate.

More than anything, Greg felt sorry for Pap. What was really going on in Pap's mind? How *aware* was Pap of his problems? Was he just pretending not to see the changes in himself, or was he truly unaware of them?

Greg remembered something a comedian had once said: "Hey, the good thing about Alzheimer's is that you're always meeting new people." The line had been funny then. It wasn't funny now.

Vicki cornered Greg not long before the party started and observed sadly, "It's all so *depressing*. I feel like this is going to be the last thing we ever do in this house. And it's not going to be fun at all."

Greg felt queasy. The stage was set; it was unavoidable now. This party was going to be a catastrophe. Someone was going to get hurt.

Ultimately, Pap didn't dress up, but he wore the hat he had pulled from the trunk, announcing that it was more than enough costume for his birthday.

The big surprise was Aunt Minnie. She rushed through the front door wearing a large bunny rabbit costume. Greg couldn't imagine what made her think that was a good idea. Her ears flapped from her head like deflated balloons. The body suit sagged in all the wrong places. Her cottontail made her look incontinent.

"Somebody hide me," she gasped. "Old Man Hennessy is after me."

"Why? Is it rabbit season?" Pap asked.

She puffed, "It's *Minnie* season. He's been trying to get me to marry him. When he saw this outfit, he went wild."

"I keep telling Hennessy to stop reading those magazines," Pap said. "They're bad for his heart."

Someone on the porch coughed, and Aunt Minnie suddenly stepped aside. "Good heavens, I almost forgot."

A man entered. Greg guessed he was probably in his early thirties, but might have been older. He was tall and lanky, with limp black hair that lay in sharp contrast to his pasty white skin. He was dressed in a white lab coat and wore large round glasses. Greg thought he looked like the dentist from a bad drama production of "Little Shop of Horrors."

"You must be Elmer Fudd," Frank said.

"Elliot, actually," the man replied. "Elmer is my brother."

Minnie quickly explained the labyrinth of family associations on Minnie's side that led to Elliot's existence, concluding with: "So he's your cousin, second or third removed."

"Removed from what?" Frank asked. "Is that your costume or are you really a doctor?"

"I'm a doctor, of sorts."

"Aha!" Pap cried out. "A doctor! So you've called for reinforcements. Well, I won't go. You'll have to drag me kicking and screaming. The neighbors will talk. They'll have pictures in the paper." Pap suddenly grabbed Elliot's hand and made a fuss over checking up his sleeves. "No secret hypodermics. No hidden sedatives."

Poor Elliot looked at Aunt Minnie helplessly.

"Cut it out, Dad," Frank said.

"I don't trust you," Pap said while he made a show of frisking Elliot. "One minute I'll be drinking some punch and the next minute I'll wind up in a round rubber room with a box of crayons."

"This is an interesting side of the family," Elliot said to Aunt Minnie.

Colleen disarmed the moment by asking for help in the kitchen. And for the next ten minutes Greg watched as his mother carefully navigated Pap and Frank away from each other.

The birthday guests began to show up. Most were Pap's age or older. Greg wound up playing doorman and helping some of them to their chairs. The women smelled of lavender and something that reminded Greg of bathroom air-freshener. The men carried the smells of hair tonic and aftershave. Some were dressed in costume, most didn't bother. Many of them seemed to know Greg and patted his hand warmly as if they'd been friends for years. Greg stammered in response, not knowing a soul.

Greg heard Pap tell anyone who asked that he was dressed like Clark Gable, because of the hat. No one believed him.

Vicki was pressed into service as the drinks girl and drifted through the crowd with a tray of white cups filled with punch and soda. Her T-shirt sleeve unrolled and the box fell to the floor. It was a box of playing cards.

At that moment Greg noticed how adult she seemed. Not so much because of her silly outfit, but because of the casual way she talked to the old folks. She didn't show any of the self-consciousness that many kids her age showed around adults. He felt a twinge of something, maybe jealousy, because she was so confident. Or maybe it was a sense of loss, because he now saw her as something other than the little squirt kid-sister he was so used to. Maybe she was growing up.

"I'll get the cake," Colleen said more to herself than anyone and went to the kitchen.

Greg wandered toward Pap and Aunt Minnie. Pap had his old address book in hand.

"I thought Martha told you to throw that out," Aunt Minnie was saying.

"She did?"

"Good heavens, Walter, don't you remember? It was one of the worst fights you two ever had. Right after you got married. Martha didn't want you to keep it, and you wouldn't give it up."

Pap nodded. "She had a jealous streak in her."

"She came to my house, crying her eyes out. She said she was never going back to you. She didn't want to be married to a playboy. It was so funny," Aunt Minnie laughed lightly. "Imagine her thinking *you* could be a playboy."

"That's not so far-fetched," Pap protested. "But she should have known that nobody could come close to her in my heart."

Greg wondered if Pap was going to regale everyone again with how he and Grandma met, but he didn't. Instead he sat back in his chair and grabbed a handful of pretzels from a bowl. He watched everyone happily, proudly. "I wish she could be here now," he said, but Aunt Minnie had already turned away to talk to someone else.

They'd been married such a long, long time, Greg mused. How did he cope with her death? Or worse, how did he cope with the time *after* her death? It was hard for Greg to imagine being alone after spending over forty years with someone. He looked around the room for some sign of her. It was as if Pap's clutter had driven her from the room, like weeds choking a garden. She was a vague memory to Greg now. Sometimes he remembered how she gave him pocket change to go buy himself some sweets from the local candy shop. Other times he saw her hunched over a table, playing gin rummy. He saw her milky white skin and small eyes, fragile fingers carefully arranging her hand of cards. She drew pictures for Greg, too. With a few strokes of a pen, she created whole scenes for his amusement: boats on the ocean, a kite in the sky, an odd-looking bear in a forest. More than any other memory, Greg saw her standing in the kitchen, her old slippers flapping against the worn linoleum as she moved between the stove and the sink—making her special pancakes for breakfast, or bread, or the crack and sizzle of her fried chicken. Did Pap think of all these things, too?

Greg watched his grandfather. Pap gazed at the small crowd of family and friends. He looked lost. And now Pap's gaze went beyond them to the room, scanning the walls and up to the ceiling, probably thinking about leaving his house. Then, as if on cue, Pap closed his eyes and shook his head.

What a terrible time for him. Gradual change was one thing; this was more like an assault. But was it so different from what Greg was experiencing? Maybe. At least Greg had choices: He could go to college or not go to college, work for awhile or even travel around the world. He could decide for himself. Pap was being *forced* to make changes.

In a glow of yellow candlelight from the birthday cake, Colleen stood in the doorway to the kitchen. "Tah dah!" she exclaimed. There was scattered applause as she sat the cake on the TV dinner tray table. "I couldn't get all the candles on here, but I've got twenty-five. You can divide it or multiply it or whatever."

"My wife the mathematician," Frank said.

"I can't eat any of that," one old woman complained. "I'll go into glucose shock just *thinking* about it."

"Go on, Walter, blow out your candles," a growly old fellow called from the back.

"We have to sing first," Colleen said, and then began the "Happy Birthday" song. Everyone's faces were bright and smiling as they sang. Pap's cheeks went a patchy red, his lips spreading into an embarrassed grin. And for a moment, Greg hoped he was wrong about the evening. Maybe it would turn out all right after all. Maybe he could relax and enjoy himself.

Pap leaned towards the candles.

"Blow them all out in one try—if you can," Frank challenged him.

"Ha." Pap leaned forward and then eyed the top of the cake. "What's this say? 'On Your Bar Mitzvah.'"

Colleen smiled and shrugged. "Thelma dropped your birthday cake, so we had to come up with a quick alternative."

"After all these years, you're finally a man," Greg said to Pap. He was feeling better, even lighthearted.

"Blow out the candles, Pap," Vicki said. "You're getting wax all over the cake."

"Make a wish," someone reminded him.

"Okay. . ." Pap took a deep breath and blew out the candles. Everyone applauded. "I didn't get my wish. I'm still old," he said.

"Now you can get a discount when you go bowling," another friend said.

Pap laughed. "I knew I lived this long for something." Then he began to cough.

From where Greg stood, it looked like Pap had sucked in some of the smoke from the candles.

As Pap continued to cough, Frank stepped closer. "Dad, are you all right?"

Pap motioned at them, his coughing getting worse, becoming wheezier.

"Would you like some water?" Colleen asked.

He nodded quickly and she went to get it.

Pap coughed and gasped more loudly, his face turning bright red. Frank patted him on the back—softly at first, then harder.

"Are you sure he's not having a heart attack?" someone asked.

Pap tried to wave Frank away and leaned forward, his hacking now wild and uncontrollable.

"Hurry with that water," Aunt Minnie called.

"Boil some water!" an ancient-looking man with a cane shouted.

From the kitchen, Greg could hear the sound of the pipes rumbling. Colleen cried out with pain; she must have kicked the pipes.

Pap's coughing and wheezing was unabated. *He's going to die,* Greg thought, but stood by numbly, not knowing what to do. "Should we call an ambulance?" he asked no one.

"I'll call!" Vicki said, racing to a phone. She put the receiver to her ear, then slammed it down. She lifted the wire, the end of it frayed and unattached to anything helpful. She grabbed another phone, but slammed it down, too. "Where is the *real* phone?" she asked with great exasperation.

"In the kitchen," Frank shouted.

"Do we need an ambulance?" Aunt Minnie asked. "Let him have some air. He just needs air."

"Greg!" Frank called out. "Air!"

Greg grabbed an old magazine and began to fan Pap.

Frank moved to the front of the chair and knelt. "Put your head between your legs," Frank said. Pap looked at him wild-eyed.

Colleen limped across the room with a glass of water. Pap, who was struggling to breathe, took the glass and gulped the water down.

Vicki entered, carrying a phone book. She riffled through the pages. "Would ambulance be under 'a' for ambulance or 'p' for paramedic?" she asked. "9-1-1 was busy."

Frank gestured to Elliot, who stood nearby with his drink in hand and a breadstick hanging from his mouth. "Elliot, you're a doctor! Do something!"

Elliot looked shocked. "Actually—"

Minnie said, "Frank, he's not—"

"*Just do something!*" Frank commanded.

"But I'm a veterinarian," Elliot said, stepping forward.

Pap suddenly took in some air, long and deep, and held up his hands in surrender. Finding his voice, he rasped, "I'm fine! I'm fine!"

"Thank God," Elliot said and returned to his breadstick. "I haven't worked on people in years."

"And you're not starting with me!" Pap growled, then said to Greg, "You're going to give me pneumonia if you keep that up."

Greg, lost in the excitement, had forgotten how frantically he'd been fanning the air. He now blushed and put the magazine down. A nervous laugh of relief went through the small gathering.

"Well. . . ," Frank began, but Pap suddenly turned on him.

"And what were *you* trying to accomplish?" Pap asked.

"What?"

"Beating me half to death, then telling me to put my head between my legs—"

"What was I supposed to do? You were choking to death," Frank said.

"I wasn't choking to death."

"Sure looked like it to me," Frank insisted.

"You overreacted. You *always* overreact," Pap said, his voice rising. "A man coughs, and you think he's dying. A man gets forgetful, and you want to lock him away."

Well, Greg thought, *here it comes. . .*

Frank's jaw dropped. "Wait a minute. *Who* was overreacting? Since when is it overreacting to worry about you? This could have been a real emergency."

"But it wasn't."

"But it could have been," Frank said, making his case. "And then what?"

"Then nothing," Pap said.

"But what if it was?" Frank persisted. "What if you really were choking?"

Pap seemed to know what Frank's question was leading to. "So what if I really was choking? With you running around like a bunch of idiots, I probably would have died. *Alone,* I might have stood a chance to survive."

Vicki returned with the phone book. "The phone number for the ambulance was disconnected. Is there somewhere else I should try?"

Pap waved towards her. "See? I could have walked to the hospital in that amount of time. I don't need your or anyone else's help. And I'm not moving out of my house."

Colleen stepped between Frank and Pap and held up a large, very threatening knife. "Let's cut the cake!"

∞

THE PARTY DIDN'T RECOVER after Pap's choking incident and the brief exchange between Pap and Frank. Pap's friends had their cake quietly. Greg watched as they scratched their heads and leaned toward one another to ask quietly if Walter was moving or if Frank was throwing him out of the house. A couple of them confessed in whispers that they'd noticed the changes in Pap's behavior over the past several months and had known all along it would come to this.

Eventually the only ones left were the Reynolds family, Aunt Minnie, and Elliot, who still walked around with a confused expression on his face.

"Well, I hope you're satisfied," Pap finally said to Frank. "The whole town gets to see how my son treats his father on his big day."

Frank slumped onto the couch. "That's right. I'm the bad guy. Somehow, and I don't know how, your coughing fit was all my fault."

"Nobody said you're a bad guy," Colleen said.

Frank lay back and put an arm over his eyes. "You're a horse doctor, Elliot. *You* tell him what they do with old horses. They're put out to pasture where someone can take care of them."

Elliot cleared his throat nervously. "Actually, we shoot them and send them to the glue factory."

Frank sat up on his elbows. "You do what?"

"There's your answer," Pap said, folding his arms. "Are you satisfied?"

"Could we save this for tomorrow?" Colleen asked.

"Fine with me," Frank said. But he clearly couldn't resist getting in the last word. "But I want to go on record that I am *not* an overreactor."

"Yes, you are," Pap said. "You always were—even when you were a kid. You worried and fretted and then turned into a basket case when things went wrong."

"Aunt Minnie, help me with this," Frank pleaded. "This isn't my doing."

Minnie shook her head. "This is a family matter. Just tell me where to forward the mail."

"You *are* family—and it's because of *your* mail that we even started this discussion," Frank reminded her.

Aunt Minnie turned to Elliot. "I think it's time we went home."

"Now wait a minute," Frank said, sitting up. "Don't hang me out to dry. Didn't you write to us that you were worried? Didn't you tell us about the visits to the doctor?"

"Well, *Benedict* Minnie?" Pap asked with a steely gaze.

Minnie put on her coat. "I might have."

Frank pressed on, "Come on, Aunt Minnie. Tell him that he needs to get out of this house and get professional care before he hurts himself or someone else."

Pap was aghast. "Before I hurt myself or someone else? I'm a danger to society now?"

"Maybe we should all go to bed now," Colleen suggested.

"I'm a *danger* now?" Pap asked, ignoring her. "You're overreacting again."

"All right," Frank began, rising to the bait. "Tell me what happened to your car."

Pap looked at him with a blank expression.

"You've been in some kind of accident," Frank said. "What happened?"

Pap shook his head. "I don't know what you're talking about."

"My point exactly," Frank said, getting to his feet. "This is what we're worried about. This is what I'm *overreacting* to."

"Let's talk about this rationally. Like grown-ups," Minnie said.

"Oh, please," Colleen appealed to them. "Do we have to do this tonight?"

Frank held up his hands in a gesture of resignation. "Can't you see that my father *wants* to talk about it now? Why do you think he's been jabbing at me all day? That's why he keeps pushing me."

"I'm pushing *you!"* Pap said. "Now that's the pot calling the kettle black! You've been pushing ever since you got here. From the minute you walked in, you wanted to talk me out of this house. That's how you are. It's how you've always been. You're pushy and bossy. Just ask anyone in this room."

"Don't change the subject," Frank said.

"I'm serious," Pap said. "Ask your family if you're pushy and bossy. You'll see."

"Okay, if that's what you want." Frank turned to his family. "Am I pushy and bossy?" He gestured to Colleen. "Well?"

"He's hitting your buttons, Frank," Colleen said quietly. "Don't you see?"

"Just humor him and answer the question. He said I'm overreacting, and I'm pushy and bossy. Is he right?"

Colleen sighed. "Oh, Frank. Stop it. This isn't about you, remember?"

"That's not an answer," Pap said, wagging a finger at Frank as if he'd just scored a point somehow.

Frank was now on his feet, pacing. His jaw was tightening and loosening, tightening and loosening. He was visibly trying to control his feelings.

"Ask Greg," Pap said. "Ask *him* if you're pushy and bossy."

"Me?" Greg croaked.

"No," Frank said firmly. "You're trying to change the subject from the real problem here."

But Pap wouldn't let it drop. "Go on, Greg. Tell him the truth."

Greg wished his chair would swallow him up so he wouldn't have to be part of this scene. But it wasn't going to be that easy.

Pap persisted. "Are you a man or a mouse, Greg? Are you going to let him in on your little secret?"

Greg felt his cheeks flush as Frank turned to face him. "What's he talking about?"

Greg felt cornered, all eyes in the room on him. His mind reeled. "Dad . . . well, sometimes you get locked into your own point of view and it's . . . hard to talk to you when you get like that."

Frank gazed at his son. "And?"

"You have to realize that all these changes are . . . are scary," Greg said carefully. "And sometimes things aren't going to change the way you want them to."

"Very diplomatically put," Aunt Minnie said.

Frank obviously wasn't as impressed. "Tell me something I don't know, Greg," he said. "We're scared by a few changes, I know that. We'd be crazy not to be. I'm scared about losing my job. I admit that. Why? Because I *know* I'll wind up wearing a paper hat and selling hamburgers at Biffy Barf's or some other grease pit. And Pap is scared of moving out of the house he's lived in for over forty years. Right? I don't need you to tell me that."

Greg felt a spring of anger well up inside of him. Didn't his father realize he was trying to sympathize? Didn't his father see that he was trying to help? His throat burned as he said, "I'm not only talking about your job or what's happening with Pap. I'm talking about other things."

"Like what?"

Greg thought the room was now terribly hot. He felt beads of sweat form on his neck and face. He could cross the line and say what he really wanted to say—or he could retreat now and leave the moment alone. "You know, things that have to do with other members of our household."

Vicki, who had been trying to scrub the fake tattoos off, now chose to speak. "Like getting my belly button pierced."

Frank shot her a silencing look, then said to Greg, "You're going to have to be a little clearer. What are you talking about?"

"I'm talking about my decision not to go to college."

Colleen instinctively put a hand to her mouth. Vicki lowered her face into her hands and groaned.

Aunt Minnie leaned to Pap and said, "Nice going, Walter."

"The boy needs to be honest with his father," Pap said simply.

Frank didn't take his eyes off of Greg. "You *what?*" he asked.

"Remember, Dad, we're grown-ups here," Greg said, wishing more than ever that he'd run away from home earlier in his life.

"You're not a grown-up," Frank stated.

Aunt Minnie gestured to Elliot. "We should be hopping along now. It's time for all old rabbits to go back to their dens."

Elliot nodded to everyone. "It was nice meeting you."

From the door, Minnie said, "Good night. If I hear shots, I'll come back."

"*I* won't," Elliot said. "Good night."

Greg braced himself as Frank sat back down on the couch. Frank folded his hands on his knees and spoke with measured calmness. "Greg, you have to go to school. What kind of future will you have without it?"

"School's overrated, Dad. There are other things I want to do."

"Like what, for example?" Frank asked. "I've been to the unemployment office. It's no thrill."

"I want to think about my life, decide what to do. Maybe travel for awhile."

"Great. *There's* a solid plan."

Now Greg was on his feet and pacing. "Dad, can you think in terms of something other than a *solid plan?* Just once, can we allow for something that isn't a *solid plan?*"

"Not when it comes to your future, no."

"*My* future," Greg snapped back, his courage growing. "You said it. It's *mine,* not yours."

"Don't be childish."

"Why is it that whenever I insist on doing what *I* want to do, it's childish?"

"You just answered your own question."

Greg stood behind a wingback chair, as if he needed it for cover. "Look, this isn't something we can argue about. I'm laying off for a semester, maybe a year, to be childish or whatever you want to call it."

Frank stood up and moved towards the chair. "Fine. That's fine. You don't want college—then try your hand at the real world. It's all yours. But don't think you'll use any of *my* hard-earned money to do it."

"Frank—," Colleen began.

It was too late. Greg watched his father get closer until only the chair separated them. If it wasn't for that, they would have been eyeball to eyeball. Greg kept his eyes locked on his father, not daring to flinch or retreat.

"Here's the deal," Frank said. "If you go to college, I'll do everything I can to help you. If you want to waste your time and *not* go to college, then you can't sponge off of me. It's that simple. I didn't work all these years to watch you throw it all away."

Greg stared at his father. He hadn't expected it to go this far—to reach an ultimatum. But there it was: *Pap had pushed Dad's buttons, and now he's pushing mine.* He bit the inside of his mouth and said as calmly and as coldly as he could, "All right. I'll give it some thought." He turned and went to the closet next to the front door. He pulled out his jacket. It shook in his hands.

"Where are you going?" Colleen asked, alarmed.

"I want to get some fresh air," he answered. His heart pounded in his chest as he zipped up his coat. He fixed his eyes on the floor, not daring to look anywhere else; his gaze focused on a bit of faded and frayed carpet in the corner. There was something else to be said, but he didn't know what it was.

"Now, now—there's no need to get overdramatic about this," Pap said. "Take your coat off, Greg."

Greg shook his head. "I want to take a walk."

"Stick around, let's talk it out," Pap insisted. Greg turned to him. Pap now looked worried, as if he suddenly realized he'd gone too far. His voice had a slight tremble to it. "Frank, talk to your son."

"And say what?" Frank challenged him. "I'm the overreactor, remember? I'm pushy and bossy. You've made that point crystal clear tonight."

Pap held up his hands. "Okay, maybe I got carried away. I do that sometimes. It's so easy to—what did you call it, Colleen?— push your buttons. That's all. I was just pushing your buttons. Your mother used to get after me about that. You and I would fight, and she always knew the right words to fix things right up."

"That's right, Dad. Joyful memories," Frank said sarcastically.

Pap lowered his head and continued as if he hadn't heard. He said softly, "I wish Mary could be here. She'd know what to do. She always did."

Frank cocked his head as if he hadn't heard right. "Mary?"

The change in Frank's tone seemed to catch Pap's attention. He looked up. "Yes. Mary."

"Mary *who?*" Frank asked.

"Your mother," Pap replied, looking at Frank as if he'd just turned into a canary.

Greg felt a tight ball form in the pit of his stomach. He wanted to leave. But his feet didn't move. They couldn't.

"You mean *Martha*, don't you?" Frank asked.

Pap frowned at him. "I said Mary, and I meant Mary. What's wrong with you?"

Frank turned away from Pap. He shook his head and sighed heavily.

"What's wrong with everybody?" Pap asked, looking at each of them.

Colleen said gently, "You meant to say Martha, I'm sure."

Pap gaped at her. "No, I didn't."

"Mom's name was *Martha*, not Mary," Frank said.

"You're senile."

Frank faced his father again. "Don't you think I know my own mother's name?"

"She was *my* wife before she was *your* mother."

"And her name was Martha."

"Let it go, Dad," Greg said from the door. But he knew his father wouldn't.

"Where's that stuff we brought down from the attic? The framed marriage certificate?" Frank asked.

It was sitting on the table next to Vicki. She handed it over to him.

Frank took a quick look at it and then gave it to his father.

Pap wouldn't look at the certificate at first, and Greg now reached for the door. He'd known that someone would get hurt—now it looked as if everyone would, especially Pap.

"Martha," Pap whispered, and his look was so crestfallen that Greg thought he might cry. "I'm looking right at it, but it still doesn't seem familiar."

"That happens to me in geometry all the time," Vicki said with a forced smile.

"I'm going to tidy up now," Pap stood up and said quietly.

"I'll do it," Colleen offered.

"No," Pap said firmly. "I want to."

They watched as Pap walked to the kitchen. Greg pushed open the storm door and headed out into the crisp autumn night.

∞

Pap carried half-empty cups of punch and crumb-covered paper plates to the wastebasket. He had to bite his lower lip to keep from talking to himself, a habit he'd formed while living alone for such a long time. The family had gone upstairs.

Now he wished he hadn't insisted on cleaning up. After only a few trips between the kitchen and the living room he felt tired, ready for bed. He thought he'd like to crawl under the covers and read himself to sleep. He was in the middle of a Zane Grey. What was it called? He couldn't think of the title.

He worked hard to fight off a growing sense of panic. Tired ... forgetful ... exactly what Dr. Janssen had warned him would happen. How many times had he gone to the store for milk and come back empty-handed? Or gone out for bread, thinking he'd forgotten it, bought some, then returned home to a cabinet full of it? In the past several months that had happened a lot. He didn't dare tell anyone about the stack of unpaid bills he'd shoved in the closet. It wasn't that he didn't have the money to pay them, but that writing checks had become so difficult. He couldn't remember which way a seven turned, or which line was for numbers and which line was for his signature.

Frank had brought up Pap's car accident, but what Frank didn't know was that Pap had stopped driving a long time ago—after he'd lost the keys. That's why it sat parked halfway in the garage. He couldn't find the keys to pull it all the way in. Now he worried that it would snow and the garage would be ruined.

Until the unfortunate ending, he'd thought he was doing well at the party. Frank and Colleen would never have guessed how traumatized he'd been at the thought of all those people coming over.

He had stood in the bathroom that morning scheming ways to get out of it. Standing with his hands clenching the side of the sink bowl, he had wanted to lock the door and not let anyone into his house. Then he'd felt the gathering warmth around his crotch and the cool sting down his legs, and he realized he'd wet himself. How could he go to a party?

But Frank had saved the day without even knowing it. Frank had talked to him about moving out of the house, and that had given him something to focus on. His anger, that is. Pap had been furious all day and all through the party. Frank had no right telling him what to do.

Pap shoved everything into the wastebasket and then, almost instinctively, dug into the trash to pull out some silverware. He'd been doing a lot of that lately, too.

It was his *big* mistake that now preyed on his mind. How could he confuse Martha's name with Mary? She was the one thing in his life that he couldn't forget. There wasn't a minute in any hour of any day that he didn't think about her. Sometimes he prayed that God would let her haunt him—just let him see her every once in awhile. Better still, let her talk to him. He talked to her often enough.

Even now, as he walked back to the living room, he was conversing with her. *This is what you missed by leaving too soon,* he said. To think that he could look her in the face and not know her name. *What would you say? What would you say if you found me trying to shovel snow in August?* Perhaps he could cope with all those things if she were there. He hated growing old without her. He resented her for leaving him behind to face this problem alone.

But you're not alone, she would say. *The same God who saw you through your youth will see you through your old age. You must have faith.*

Easy for you to say, Pap argued. *You're not dealing with any of this.*

Pap felt a surge of disappointment. What had happened to the wise elder he thought he'd be? Once upon a time he'd envisioned himself as a white-haired sage who would have people knocking on his door for advice all the time. *They knocked on my door, all right. And asked me to give up my Sunday school class.*

Why was this happening to him? Was it something he had done wrong as a young man? He'd lived a clean life, hadn't he? No cussing, no alcohol, no tobacco, no firearms. Maybe he *should* have messed with all those things, then he would have died at the age of fifty and not had to worry about this. Was this the end of a righteous life? Was this God's reward—slowly going through his body like it was an old house, and turning off the lights, one at a time?

Pap looked around him. He was sitting in his favorite chair, but he couldn't remember when he had sat down. Had he been asleep? He'd come into the living room, but couldn't remember now why he was there.

A blast of cool air covered him. He thought he heard rain. Then he realized that someone had opened the front door. Greg stepped in, quietly closed the door, hung up his coat in the closet, and headed for the stairs.

He doesn't know I'm here, Pap thought. *Maybe I'm not. Maybe I've disappeared.*

But Greg suddenly stopped at the foot of the stairs and tilted his head. "Pap?"

"Greg?"

"Why are you sitting in the dark?"

Pap looked around. He hadn't realized he was sitting in the dark. "I was just thinking. What time is it?"

"2:15."

"Don't *you* start."

"It is!" Greg tried to show him the face of his watch by the light from the lamp at the top of the stairs.

"Where've you been?" Pap asked.

"Walking around," Greg replied. "I never realized how quiet a town could be in the middle of the night. The diner on Route 40 was open, though."

"It never closes. They get a lot of business from the trucks passing through. I don't know what they're going to do when they put in the bypass." Pap remembered when they built that diner some fifty years ago, back when Peabody had strong business with travelers in the summer—people using Route 40 on their way to somewhere or on their way back. There had been the diner and several motels back then. Now there was just the diner.

"Everything's changing, Pap."

Pap nodded sadly. "It is. Awfully fast."

Greg sat down on the couch, a shadow. Pap could almost imagine him as a little boy again. "Change isn't always bad, though," Greg said.

"No, I don't suppose it is."

"I've been doing a lot of thinking."

"About what?" Pap asked.

"Everything," Greg replied. "Mostly about moving, though."

"Ah. Moving." He bristled at the word.

"People move all the time out of comfortable situations and are very happy," Greg reasoned.

Pap squinted at his grandson. He was still a shadow on the couch, but Pap thought he could make out the whites of his eyes and teeth. "Are they happy?" Pap asked.

"I think so," Greg said. "In fact, some people say that if you live too comfortably you'll stop growing and stagnate."

"Who says that?" Pap asked. Words like "growing" and "stagnate" were the stuff of pop psychologists and advertising writers. Pap didn't trust either. "Who says living comfortably is a bad thing?"

"I don't know," Greg said, a hint of worry in his voice. "People. You know. The people who say those kinds of things."

Pap scrubbed his chin. "Are they the same people who say 'Early to bed, early to rise, makes a man healthy, wealthy, and wise'?

"I guess."

"They're not always right, you know," Pap said grumpily.

"I know. But they might be this time," Greg said. "Growth involves change, doesn't it?"

And pain, Pap thought. *Sometimes it involves pain.*

Greg spoke as if he'd come to a final conclusion. "But we have to swallow our pride and push ahead."

Pap thought about Martha again. What would she say to him now? *You have to step ahead in faith, Walter, and believe that God will see you through.* That's what she would say.

"Pap?"

"We have to step ahead in faith. God will see us through," Pap said, like an echo to the thoughts in his head. He didn't feel the truth of the words, but he believed it. He always had.

"Right," Greg said. He stood up. His voice took on a sense of urgency that Pap recognized as a hallmark of youth: passion. Pap recalled that Greg had always been that way about things: the environment, his Christianity, flossing, the evils of country and western music. Greg said, "I mean, you've gotta change, or you'll stop growing. You might as well be dead. I'm not dead. Are you?"

"I'm afraid to check. But, no, I don't think so."

"Then we have to accept change," Greg concluded.

Pap nodded. "I guess we do."

"Fine." Pap could hear him settle back down onto the couch. "That settles it, then."

"I guess it does," Pap said with a twinge of sadness. And there it was. The decision was made. "Now what about you, Greg? Have you decided what you're going to do?"

Greg paused, his voice full of confusion. "That's what I've been talking about. I'm moving out of the house to figure out what I'm going to do with my life."

"Oh," Pap said.

Greg still didn't get it. "What did you think we were talking about, Pap?"

"I'm talking about moving out of my house and going to one of those retirement places."

Greg sounded surprised. "Oh."

Pap chuckled, but there was no humor in it. He hoped that Martha was watching from somewhere, pleased with his decision.

Greg leaned forward and asked, "Are you sure?"

"Are *you* sure?" Pap challenged him, as if Greg's answer might affect his own.

"Yes," Greg replied firmly.

Pap nodded. "Then so am I."

Part Two

The Faded Flower

☙ *God, what are you doing to me?*

That's the question I've been asking for the past year or so. Colleen calls it my *refrain*. I call it my *little prayer*. Because, apart from that question, I'm not sure I'd be talking to God at all.

As a churchgoer, I feel guilty about that sometimes. About not talking to God, I mean. It was drilled into me that it's a sin to be angry with God. And not speaking to him is a heinous crime. So I feel occasional twinges of guilt where I try to pray longer prayers or read my Bible, but it doesn't help. I usually stop, feeling just as angry as I did when I started. Sometimes angrier.

Fortunately I have Lawrence Murphy around. Lawrence is a tall, distinguished white-haired gentleman who lives at The Faded Flower Retirement Community. ("One of the *lodgers*," he jokes with a wink, knowing that the word *patients* has been banned by Mr. Kimball, the director of The Faded Flower.) He reminds me that many of the Psalms were written by men who were angry with God. He also reminds me that God is big enough to endure my anger— and my silence. And he is also quick to point out that the fact that I'm trying to ignore God means that, at the very least, I haven't stopped believing in him.

But the truth is, the only reason I stopped talking to God, apart from my little question, was because he stopped talking to me. I felt our communication shut down the day I lost my job and started to lose my father.

"A little higher, Frank," says Lawrence, bringing me back to the present.

I'm standing on a ladder, mouth full of thumbtacks, pressing the end of a banner against the wall. It says *Happy Birthday!* in bright purple sparkly letters. Stars burst all around it. I mumble through my clenched lips, "Higher? Are you sure?"

Lawrence assures me he is.

I lift the banner higher. "How's that?" I ask.

Lawrence gives me a thumbs-up.

Climbing down from the ladder, I take a few steps back to see the banner for myself. The lettering on the banner had been hand-printed by Rose Caldwell, another lodger here at The Faded Flower. "No computer print-outs for Pap," she lectured me when I had the audacity to suggest the idea. "I'll take care of it," she said. And she did.

The coloring and starbursts around the letters were painted by some of The Faded Flower's other lodgers. They love my father and are happy to contribute to his seventy-sixth birthday party in some way.

"It still looks like it's hanging low on the left," I suggest to Lawrence.

"It's perfectly fine," Lawrence says genially. "Don't you trust me?"

"No, I don't," I say. "Not when it comes to hanging great art like this."

Lawrence chuckles, low and soft. It is comforting for me to have Lawrence around. He's by far the most coherent person at The Faded Flower, other than Rose. His gentlemanly looks and calm manner (a lot like Stewart Granger, Colleen says) remind me that the world is more than wrinkles, false teeth, and bedpans—something I'm inclined to forget now that I work as a caretaker here.

The two of us are standing in the Sun Room, so called because it is a recreation room with a wall of glass that faces the west side of the grounds. It was added in the late sixties to an otherwise somber and forbidding gothic mansion made of big red stone. The mansion—known as Grayson Mansion because it was built by Stephen Grayson, an oil baron—reflected the best and the worst of the Gilded Age with its maze-like corridors, dark paneling, and angular rooms. I find its opulence oppressive. And that's one of the reasons I believe the lodgers spend more time in the Sun Room than anywhere else. It's open and fresh—and is the one area that doesn't reek of disinfectant.

"Aren't you afraid your father will see the banner before his party?" Lawrence asks.

"When's the last time you saw my father out of his room?" I remind him.

Lawrence nods thoughtfully. Pap has gotten a lot worse in the ten months since we brought him to The Faded Flower. It was as if moving him into assisted living gave him an excuse to give up on life. So he has good days and bad days, but he never improves. Only the slow descent into a strange darkness of distant memories and present fears. I see it in the eyes of many of the lodgers at The Faded Flower. I'm aware it could be a look someone will see in my eyes in another twenty years. Maybe they see it now.

And, of course, it's one more thing for me to feel guilty about.

"But, honey, he hasn't become worse *because* of the move," Colleen once said to me. "I think you may have moved him just in the nick of time. There's no telling what harm he'd have done to himself if you'd left him at home."

I wanted to believe her then—but I couldn't. How could I? She is always so upbeat and optimistic about everything. When I couldn't find a job, she said it was a blessing in disguise. ("Must be a really good disguise," I snipped.) When we had to sell our own house in order to make ends meet, she said she wouldn't miss the place. She seemed *happy* to move into Pap's place here in Peabody. She said it was like coming home again.

Eventually, nearly seven months ago and with a deep sense of humiliation, I accepted a job at The Faded Flower as a handyman. Colleen thought it was God's way of bringing me closer to my father.

In fact, now that I think about it, the only change in her life that didn't get a positive response was when Greg moved out. She showed us all a brave face as he packed up his old Chevy Nova and pulled out of the driveway, but privately she shed a lot of quiet tears and prayed for him with a fervor I'd never seen before.

Greg was going off "to discover America and himself" he told us right after Pap's last birthday.

"You're five hundred years too late," I responded.

"That's so sixties," Vicki said to Greg. "Are you going to wear a headband and love beads?" But as Greg got into his car, I suspected that Vicki would have liked to go with him. Heck, for that matter, so would I. But there was a principle I was trying to uphold, so I didn't dare let him see my grudging envy. The truth is, I was still stung by the idea that Greg was using up his hard-earned college money for this escapade.

But the boy had to do what he had to do—and suffer the consequences.

I made one tiny concession in a "no hard feelings" gesture. I bought him a small model of a chopper motorcycle in the style of the one Dennis Hopper rode in *Easy Rider*. Greg laughed and put it on his dashboard. And then he was gone.

Our most recent letter from him was postmarked somewhere in New Mexico. He was working as a waiter at night and spent his days designing Websites for local companies. I have no idea when we'll see him again.

"'Helen Altman passed away on October tenth from bone cancer,'" Ed Powell, stooped and smelling of urine, announces as he walks past. He's reading from the morning newspaper. "'She is survived by her husband, Joseph, and daughters JoAnne M. and Carol and Mary, a son, Glen A. Four brothers and sisters.'"

"Be quiet!" Barry Fitzgibbons shouts irritably from across the room.

Mr. Powell reads even louder: "'Rosary will be held Sunday, October seventeenth, at the Hudson Brothers Funeral Home.'"

I remember Billy and Jamie Hudson from elementary school. They were a couple of thugs who pestered me for my lunch money nearly every day. Leave it to them to find a future in no future and still rob people in the process.

"'John Keller passed away October eighth—'"

"Quiet!" cries out Emma Dickins from her weaving table.

"Quiet yourself!" Mr. Powell shouts back and then continues. "'John Keller passed away October eighth from natural causes—'"

"What does 'natural causes' mean?'" Lawrence asks Mr. Powell. Mr. Powell looks startled by the question. Lawrence smiles. "Does that mean his death was all natural—nothing artificial, no preservatives?"

Mr. Powell is clearly confused and doesn't know how to answer. He scowls at Lawrence, then harrumphs and drops into one of the deck chairs, muttering as he continues to read to himself.

Rose Caldwell is suddenly at my elbow. She is a short, plump woman with cropped gray hair, humor-filled gray eyes, and a sharp straight nose that looks like her face is making a gesture. "It looks wonderful," she says about the banner. Her eyes dart around the room, and I know she is considering what other arrangements to make for Pap's birthday. She seems to have a great affection for Pap and wants everything to be perfect. Not that Pap will notice.

More than once I've wondered what Rose is doing at The Faded Flower. She's a strong, levelheaded, and compassionate woman who'd been in upper management at a nearby manufacturer for years. She certainly didn't seem to need assistance. But I'd heard that she'd forfeited having a family for her career and would have lived alone if she hadn't come here. She is an Angel of Energy, doing all she can to keep everyone involved and active. Some of the folks here don't always appreciate her enthusiasm and sarcastically call her the Gestapo Social Director.

"Aha!" she suddenly says, related to nothing I can see, and then races off.

"Thank you for your help, Lawrence," I say and fold up my ladder. I carry it across to the utility closet on the far side of the room, passing James and Robert as I go. They're two friends who tend to bicker like an old married couple. At the moment, Robert is showing off his new typewriter to James. It's an antique Underwood.

"But where did you get it?" James is asking impatiently, as if he'd asked the question before and never got an answer.

"Oh. This was a present from my son-in-law. So I could write," Robert replies as he starts to hunt-and-peck his way around the keyboard.

James isn't impressed. "In an age when portable computers can fit in your shirt pocket and do a heart massage on you while you catch a bus, your son-in-law bought you an old *typewriter?*"

"They cannot!" Robert protests.

"Sure they can. I read about it in a magazine just the other day."

"A portable computer that can fit in your shirt pocket?"

"Uh-huh." James taps the shirt pocket over his breast. "Right there. Snug as a bug in a rug."

"And do a heart massage on you?"

"Well . . . why not?"

"How does it penetrate the skin?"

"What?"

"To do a heart massage, it would have to penetrate the skin. That would make you bleed, which would ruin your shirt. And it would have to somehow get past your rib cage to get to your heart to give it a massage. That would be painful. Too painful to run with. I broke a rib once, so I know about these things."

"What are you saying?"

"I'm saying that there's no way you could be running to catch a bus while all these things are going on under your shirt."

"I'm only telling you what I read in a magazine."

"It's not possible." Robert waves at me. "Frank, tell him it's not possible."

The last thing you want to do is get in the middle of one of their arguments. So I shrug and say, "I think anything is possible these days."

"There," James says.

"It's not possible," Robert maintains.

I put the ladder in the closet and then walk towards the door. Veronica Talbot is there, arms spread dramatically across the doorframe. She wears a loose-fitting robe of dull yellow with a pattern of flowers. She reminds me of Norma Desmond arriving for her close-up in *Sunset Boulevard*. That may be because Veronica claims she was once a famous child film star in the silent era, but I have yet to find anyone who's ever heard of her. More remarkably, she often remembers things that happened with famous movie stars from eighty years ago, but can't recall what she did this morning.

"Hello, *darling*," Veronica says to me in a cough-syrup voice.

"Hello, Mrs. Talbot," I reply politely, hoping to get past her without a long exchange.

"Call me Veronica. Please. It's what all my friends do."

I smile indulgently. We've had this same conversation nearly every day since I went to work for The Faded Flower. "Yes, ma'am." But I won't call her Veronica. Especially since I took her up on the offer once, and she suddenly shouted at me, "How dare you call me by my first name? I am *Mrs. Talbot* to the help!"

"I remember Douglas Fairbanks once said to me. . ."

But I feign something catching my attention over her shoulder and excuse myself. I'm not interested in another story about Douglas Fairbanks. Or the *same* story about Douglas Fairbanks, I should say.

As I walk down the hall, I think again about the year since Pap's last birthday—that awful, terrible birthday—and the twists and turns of my life. There are days when I'm convinced I'll wake up in my own bed back in my old house. I'll get up and go to work at the Bradley Company and life will be what it once was; the nightmare will be over. But then there's always a reminder that brings me back to the present, like a cold wet slap in the face. Sometimes it's the feel of the overalls against my legs rather than the lighter brush of suit trousers. Sometimes it's the sound of a metal walker clacking its way down the hall. Sometimes it's the smell of urine from someone's overturned pee-bottle.

So this is what it comes down to, I often think. Like so many of the old folks around The Faded Flower, I've been stripped of almost everything I once held dear. Even my memories of my father are being taken away from me. Just like my memories of my mother, come to think of it. When I think of her now, all that comes to mind is of her in the hospital bed with the tubes coming out of her—the machine that breathed for her. I can still hear that in-and-out noise it made. Deep hisses of noise. She lay there, her body slightly moving to the rhythm of that machine. And I know that, in the future, when I think of my father I'll think of The Faded Flower. It's indelibly stamped on my brain.

"Think of the good things, Frank. *Fight* to think of the good things. Remember," Colleen once pleaded with me when we had this conversation.

Yes, the good things. Like the day Pap bought me a secondhand bike and then tried to teach me to ride. I crashed three or four times before I realized I was better off without his help. Years later I learned that Pap himself didn't know how to ride a bike.

I remember the time he caught me in the basement smoking cigarettes. He made me smoke the whole pack to teach me a lesson. I turned green and threw up all over the living room. Mom nearly killed him for that stunt.

There was also the time I fell backwards off the porch swing— I was standing on the thing though I'd been told a hundred times not to—and Pap had to carry me a mile to the doctor because the car wouldn't start and the ambulance was on another call. I got blood all over Pap's new shirt, the one he had just picked up at Sears.

The memories come fast and furious . . . but then, like a rubber band snapping into place, I'm brought back to The Faded Flower.

What are you doing to me, God? I ask again. I've been struggling with this for a year now, and I don't see the point. God's not giving me a clue. He keeps throwing changes at me with no instruction manual for dealing with them.

"Oh, get over it, Frank," Aunt Minnie once lectured me when she'd grown tired of my complaining. "So the Lord took away all your security blankets. Is that such a bad thing?"

I snorted at her and didn't answer. That's the thing about self-pity, I suppose. It closes all the doors and windows to the fresh air of better perspective. Privately I've had to admit that things haven't been as bad as they could have been. I still have Colleen and Vicki, a place to live, a job (of sorts), and my health. I can concede that with a certain amount of gratitude. I'm no Job, I know that. But if God is responsible for taking everything else away from me, would it be so much to find out the reason?

Sometimes I worry that I have too much time on my hands to think. What else is there to do while I fix a bed or adjust cupboard doors or clear leaves from the gutters? I suppose that's why I keep coming back to my refrain: *What are you doing to me, God?*

I have attempted to get qualified help. I've posed that question to Reverend Tyler, the new minister from the Methodist church. He often comes by to visit. But Reverend Tyler, a young man with a keen expression and unfashionably long hair, only shrugs. "It's not for me to say," is his answer. "You're on a pretty wild spiritual journey, and it wouldn't be right for me to guess at God's intentions."

One day I got annoyed and shouted, "You're a minister, for crying out loud! If *you* can't guess, then who can?"

He smiled. "Beats me."

"Then what am I supposed to do?" I asked.

Reverend Tyler shrugged again. "Look, all I know is that we have a choice to make about what we believe. You can believe that God doesn't exist. You can believe that he exists, but he's apathetic and doesn't care about your problems. Worse, you can believe that he exists and is maliciously causing your problems for his own warped pleasure. Or you can believe that he exists and loves you—and your problems are somehow a mysterious extension of that love. That's all I can say."

"Thanks a lot," I said sarcastically. But in spite of all that, I like Reverend Tyler—or Andy, as he prefers to be called—and shortly after moving back to Peabody I found myself helping out with odds and ends at the church. A quick favor here and a little job there. Before I realized what was happening, I'd started attending on Sunday mornings with Colleen and Vicki. I don't know why. The place is too hot in the summer and too cold in the winter and the wooden pews hurt my butt and the choir is made up of a few diehards who can hardly hold a tune and, to be honest, Andy is better to listen to in person than he is when preaching from the pulpit. Yet Sunday after Sunday I go.

Colleen occasionally teases me about going, since I insist I'm still not speaking to God. I tell her it's an excuse to wear a suit and tie again. She doesn't believe me.

"You and the Lord are in cahoots, and you don't even realize it," Colleen says.

The Lord. I've noticed that Colleen has started using that phrase, just like Aunt Minnie. It seems so old-fashioned somehow. So Peabody-like. Reverend Tyler (Andy, I mean) always refers to God as *God,* as if he's been taught in seminary that a folksy familiarity with God's titles is inappropriate. Frankly, I like the detached respect of *God.* Lately, though, Andy has taken to calling God "our Heavenly Father," so maybe he's loosening up after all.

Andy often comes to see Pap and always smuggles in a Three Musketeers bar for him. Until Andy came along, I had no idea my father had such a weakness for chocolate. Three Musketeers bars in particular. So when I slip into Pap's room after escaping from Madam Movie Queen, I'm not terribly surprised to see one sitting on the end table next to Pap's favorite chair—a brown and green wingback. The chair is one of the few reminders my father has of his old home. He rarely sits in it now, I've noticed. Lately he's been sitting in a wheelchair. It's a mystery. It isn't that he can't walk anymore, but he seems to have lost interest in the process since he fell down a couple of months ago.

"Dad?" I call out. Pap's room, by most standards, is pretty comfy. If the bed wasn't so clearly hospital-like, the room might have looked like a one-bedroom apartment. It has a small living area with a television, the sleeping area, and a kitchenette with a sink, a small fridge, a stove, and even a dishwasher. Large signs hang on the drawers and doors labeled "Plates" and "Food" and "Utensils." Otherwise, Pap wouldn't remember where to look for things. There are also French doors that lead out to a patio, though they are usually kept locked so that Pap won't go wandering without an escort. Right now the doors are open. Cool autumn air slips in, and I can see the rear grounds of the estate beyond. The trees have shed their leaves, but the grass is still green. It's downright beautiful.

This is nothing to complain about, I think every time I go into Pap's room. But I also remember that we've paid dearly for it, mostly from the sale of my house and some cashed-in life insurance.

Pap complains about the room. A lot.

"Like father, like son," Vicki once jabbed.

I head for the patio, wondering if Pap is with someone outside, when I hear a toilet flush on the other side of the bathroom door. Now I wonder who is in the bathroom, and who had opened the patio doors. It gives me a twinge of worry. I imagine innocent visitors excusing themselves to use the toilet, and my father, unwatched for just a moment, wanders out the doors and takes a stroll—and winds up lost somewhere in Peabody.

My worries are eased when Aunt Minnie comes in from the patio carrying a large plastic bag.

"Oh, hello, Frank. I thought I'd slip out while your father was in the *you know.*"

I smile at her generation's inability to use words like *toilet,* because they're indiscreet. I kiss her cheek and ask, "But what are you doing here?"

"It's his birthday, isn't it?"

"But the party isn't until later."

"I wanted to wish him a happy birthday before the confusion of the party."

I hook a thumb towards the bathroom. "How is he today? I haven't had a chance to see him until now."

"I think he may have a fever," she says, concerned. I see afresh how much she has aged since Pap came to The Faded Flower. There are new lines around her eyes and mouth. Or maybe they aren't new—maybe they're just deeper than they were before.

"I'll tell Dr. McCall," I promise.

The bathroom door opens and Pap, in the wheelchair, pushes himself out into the room. He sees Minnie and me talking and frowns. "What are you saying over there?" he asks as he adjusts a hat on his head. It's the same hat he found in a trunk in the attic a year ago. "You're saying something," he says, his tone a warning. In the last month or so he's become paranoid that people are talking about him. It's hard to know what to say since we are, in fact, talking about him.

"I was telling Frank that I think you have a fever. Your forehead is hot," Aunt Minnie explains.

"Of course my forehead is hot. It's hot in here. If you want cold, then check my feet," Pap replies.

I hold up the Three Musketeers bar. "Was Reverend Tyler here to see you?"

Pap wheels closer. "Yes, he was and put that down. It's mine."

"Did you have a nice visit?" I ask.

"I don't like that boy. Not one bit."

"Yes, you do," Aunt Minnie reminds him.

"He keeps threatening to let the air out of my tires," Pap complains.

Aunt Minnie *tsks* at Pap. "I'm sure he's only joking."

"He stole my watch, too."

"No, he didn't," I explain for the umpteenth time. "I took it to the jeweler's to be fixed. Remember?"

I can tell by my father's expression that he doesn't remember. "What's in the bag?" he asks Minnie.

Minnie smiles coyly. "A few things."

"Toilet paper? Did you bring toilet paper?" he asks. "I hate the toilet paper they give us here. It's made by a sandpaper company in Buffalo."

"I brought some." Aunt Minnie takes out a package of toilet paper and holds it up like a trophy. I take it from her to put it away. "I got you a new toothbrush, too," she says as if offering him a new toy.

"A new toothbrush?"

"You said the other one made your gums bleed. This one will work if you use the end with the brush." Aunt Minnie hands over the toothbrush to him.

Pap nods appreciatively. "Did you have a good drive here? The roads were okay?"

"They were fine."

"It rained all morning, you know. I was afraid the roads would be wet."

It hasn't rained at all this morning, and I nearly say so. But then I think better of it and say nothing.

Aunt Minnie pats him on the shoulder reassuringly. "Not a thing to worry about. The roads were dry as a bone." She takes a wrapped present out of the bag and hands it to him. "Here. Happy birthday." She kisses him on the cheek as he takes it.

Pap looks at it with undisguised suspicion. "What's this?"

"Open it."

Pap studies it for a moment and then puts it aside. "Maybe I'll wait."

"I'm sorry," Aunt Minnie suddenly says, remembering herself. "How about if I open it for you?"

Before Pap can answer and lose his sense of dignity, Minnie takes the present and carefully undoes the ribbon. She then opens the wrapping and the box inside. "Here you go. It's a large-print edition of the Bible."

"Oh. How nice," Pap says with a childlike clap of his hands. "This is wonderful. Do I need this?"

"Yes. So you can read at night before you go to sleep."

Pap frowns. "Where's my old Bible?"

"You gave it to Greg. Remember? When you moved," I say as I lean against the back of the sofa. I can feel a spring poking me in the backside.

"Oh. Yes. I moved." Pap looks at Minnie, his expression filled with bewilderment. "I didn't like moving, did I, Minnie?"

"I don't think you did," she affirms.

"But it's okay now," Pap says with a crooked smile.

"I'm glad you think so."

This is how he is now. Moody and suspicious one minute and childlike the next.

"Do they miss me at the Senior Citizen's Social?" he asks.

Aunt Minnie now sits down in the chair and makes herself comfortable. "I told you that we do. Nobody could play charades like you."

"Or checkers."

"Nobody *wants* to play checkers like you," Aunt Minnie says quickly, and I laugh.

"Thank you," Pap says.

My pager vibrates against my side. I glance down at it. Colleen has phoned. "I have to go," I say and make for the door.

Aunt Minnie waves at me, then asks my dad, "Have you been out for a stroll yet?"

"You mean a *ride*. No."

"Then let's go." Aunt Minnie moves behind the wheelchair and pushes Pap towards the patio doors. It won't be much of a ride, I know. Generally, Aunt Minnie takes him out onto the patio, then brings him back in again.

"Minnie, why don't you move here to live? We could have a lot of fun," I hear Pap say.

"I can't now, Walter. I'm having the dining room repainted."

"Oh."

Aunt Minnie smiles at me just before she disappears through the doors onto the patio.

I head for a small closet in the back of the building. It's my workroom. I pick up the phone and dial home. Colleen picks up and says hello in a way that makes me hope she knew it was me. I don't think I like the idea of her talking in such a sultry manner to strangers. She starts to tell me about the arrangements for the party, and I'm trying to decide how to break my news to her.

"I've been thinking about it," I say to her as diplomatically as I can. "I'm not sure a surprise party is such a good idea."

"Why not?"

"I'm afraid he'll have a heart attack right in front of everyone."

"Then we'll serve his birthday cake at the viewing," she replies without missing a beat.

"Are you trying to put a positive spin on the possible death of my father?"

"It's been a positive day."

"Oh?"

I can almost hear her smile through the phone lines. "I have a couple of surprises for you."

"Uh-oh," I say. "Surprises in our family are usually bad news."

She is still smiling, I know, as I hear her moving paper around. "There's a letter here from Cohen & Marx Publishing in Baltimore. It was forwarded from our old address."

"Cohen and Marx?" I ask. Cohen & Marx was a small publishing company that specialized in paramedic training materials. I vaguely remember applying there after I'd been let go from Bradley. They had no openings for me then. "I wonder what they want."

"Do you want me to open it and see?"

"Sure, go ahead."

I can hear her slicing the letter open. "It's from … Rory Zemeckis."

The name means nothing to me.

Colleen gasps. "He wants you to contact them. They're revamping their human resources department and want you to go in for an interview."

"You're kidding." My heart skips a beat. I'm wanted for a job interview!

Colleen sounds puzzled. "Human resources?"

"That's just another name for *personnel*," I explain and my mind races. I try to remember who Rory Zemeckis is. Suddenly it clicks. I'd met Rory at a seminar a couple of years ago. We'd talked about trends in hiring and the impact of conglomerations on smaller businesses. It seems to me we had connected in a friendly, professional sort of way. I wonder what made him think of me now? But then I don't care about the answer, it's enough to be asked. "Wow," I say with my usual eloquence, trying to ignore the shot of adrenaline that pumps through my body.

Colleen gasps again. "There's a note written at the bottom."

"Well?"

Colleen suddenly laughs.

"What's wrong?" I ask. I have to pose the question repeatedly before she calms down enough to answer.

"The note says, 'My sister Sally Quinten sends her regards.'"

"Sally Qui—?" I begin, and then the name registers. "Spooky Sally?" I shout into the phone.

Colleen laughs again.

"Spooky Sally," I say again, my voice getting soft. I remember well her vision or picture or whatever you call them she'd had about me. She once said I would be living near my father again. And now, as then, I get goose-pimply. "She gives me the creeps."

"This time she may be giving you a job," Colleen says. "Or the Lord is."

"Well, we'll see about that," I say, my tone flat. The good news doesn't seem as good any more. I resent the feeling of being manipulated by Sally, even if it is on behalf of God.

Colleen clearly knows what I'm thinking and says, "She must have mentioned you to her brother. That's all. He wouldn't have written if he didn't think you were qualified for the job. You once sent them a resume, didn't you?"

I nod, forgetting that I'm talking to her on the phone. "Yes," I add. I shake off the bizarre feelings that Sally's name conjures up. Why should I care where the job opportunity comes from? Why not be grateful? It's a new chance—and maybe a fresh beginning. "Please bring the letter when you come for the party," I say. I'm about to hang up when I think to ask: "Oh—and what's the other surprise?"

"I'll bring that when I come, too."

We say our good-byes, and I grab my toolbox for a little job at the front of the building. As I walk I think about the letter. Somebody may want me again. I may be able to go back to work in a real office with real businesspeople. This is a real turning point.

Just as quickly, I find myself thinking something else: *Don't get your hopes up. It's possible that the job has already been filled, since the letter went to our old address and time has gone by.* Suddenly I could kick myself for not getting the phone number from Colleen and calling Rory right away. Obviously my old professional instincts have been dulled by the past year. I consider finding a phone to call her right away, but I don't. I feel nervous. What if my old professional instincts have completely dried up?

I press on to the front hall of The Faded Flower. It is a remarkable oak paneled room that still holds its former grandeur. It's easy to imagine the tuxedoed and bejeweled people entering for the parties oil baron Stephen Grayson once held here. In they would come through the large front door with the stained glass center. The guests would place their cards on the silver tray that still adorned the gigantic round oak table along with the antique vase filled with the day's cuttings of flowers. Directly beyond the table they'd admire the broad red-carpeted stairs leading up to a landing where more stained glass windows with a flower-type design splashes blues and greens down onto the stairs and ornate banister. No doubt many of the guests would wish they could ascend those stairs to see the many rooms on the second floor. But few of them would. They'd be guided into the main drawing room off to the side with its dark wood paneling and hand-carved hearth and crystal chandelier. Oh, the glory of days gone by.

Today, however, the wheelchair carrier that now lines one side of the stairs is acting up. I hunch over it with a screwdriver and open the power box. I fiddle around, trying to figure out why the mechanism has ground to a halt, and realize that I'll have to call in an electrician. I hate to do that. I feel as if spending The Faded Flower's money is the same as spending my own. But I also know that I'll never be able to fix the stupid thing.

Why not call in an electrician? I argue with myself. *Splurge a little, live a little, go wild.* I'm amused at the idea, as if calling in some help is the same as indulging in dinner at the best restaurant in town.

Do it, I think. It's a day to celebrate. Somebody wants me. Somebody back in the world I thought I'd left behind is inviting me to return. This is something to have a party about. I won't have to fix anything around here ever again.

Sitting on a stair, I imagine myself back in an office, attending meetings, drinking cups of coffee with my coworkers (instead of carrying a thermos from home—the coffee here is *awful*), writing business letters, talking on the phone to strangers, shaking hands, and interpreting employment trends. I look down at the screwdriver I'm holding in my hand. It's shaking. Boy, I'm really nervous. My insecurity now outpumps my adrenaline. I've been out of the game for a year. Can I go back and be as successful as I was before?

I shrug off the thought. Of course I'll be successful. I'll rise to the occasion and show them that I haven't gone rusty.

I stand up and suddenly want to laugh. "Do you see?" I say to God. "In spite of your scheming, your tricks to knock me out of the running, I'm going back. You just watch me."

Only as I'm putting the screwdriver back into the toolbox does it occur to me that maybe this is God's long-delayed answer to my prayer. Maybe God has finally come through for me.

Or has he?

I kneel next to the toolbox and rub my forehead. My head aches. Is this an answer to prayer? I suppose I've always assumed that my current situation was temporary, that whatever penance I had to pay for whatever sin I'd committed to bring this about would eventually end. One way or another I would go back to where I belong. But now I have to wonder. Where do I belong?

Again, I try to shrug off the questions and doubts. "You think too much," my mother once complained to me. And now I believe she was right.

The door springs open with a burst of cold air and dry leaves. Colleen and Vicki arrive carrying a couple of trays of goodies they've baked together at home. They are red-cheeked and excited, jabbering like two best friends.

"There's more in the car," Colleen tells me breathlessly as they head down the hall for the kitchen.

I step outside into the dying afternoon sunshine. I shiver at the evening air. Where has the day gone? I hadn't realized it was getting so late.

I go to the car, the trunk lid yawning at me. The floor is littered with trays of baked goods. I juggle two and turn back towards The Faded Flower. I have to pause. In the dusk, the mansion looks very cozy with its large ivy-covered red stones. Dull yellow lights burn in some of the windows, and I can see figures moving. The hall lights, which are timed to turn on now, highlight the light green Victorian wallpaper. I see Colleen and Vicki enter the front hall again, returning to help. Vicki is laughing and talking excitedly about something. It occurs to me that, of everyone who's been impacted by the circumstances of the past year, Vicki seems to be the one who's benefited from it. Since Pap's last birthday, she has moved gracefully into womanhood, without any of the angst or bad attitudes her old friends used to have. She gives every impression of liking Peabody. Heck, she even seems to like all the folks at The Faded Flower. They all treat her like a granddaughter. Even more surprising, she acts as if she enjoys having me and Colleen around. My work schedule is so flexible that we can often sneak off to a matinee as soon as she gets out of school, or we meet for lunch and have a picnic in the park. And, come to think of it, there isn't much that she and Colleen don't do together.

As they come out, I wonder what the two of them think about my potential job offer. Are they for it or against it? Colleen betrayed nothing on the phone, not that I gave her the chance to say one way or the other.

As she passes me, Colleen holds up the letter and then tucks it into my back pocket. She kisses me quickly on the cheek. "You better get those trays inside before you drop them."

I realize I'm still standing there like a dolt, balancing the two trays. "But what about it?" I ask Colleen, drawing her into the middle of my thoughts. "Is this a good thing?"

She knows what I'm talking about. "Let's discuss it later. Right now we have to get ready for Pap's party."

"*Everybody's* coming," Vicki says happily. "We invited everyone we could think of. Even Pap's old friends from the church."

I let Vicki catch up with me as we walk to the kitchen. "You like it here, don't you?" I ask her.

"In the nursing home?"

"*Here*. In Peabody."

Vicki nods as she tries to fit a tray into one of the large industrial refrigerators. I eye her for a moment. Yeah, she's growing up quickly. Her face is losing its round babyness. Her body is changing its proportions. She doesn't squeak and shout anymore. Now she speaks in the same level tones as her mother. The frantic pace she kept in our old house is gone. She's still active, she has her friends from school and church, but she is more relaxed. I can't remember the last time she's asked about getting a tattoo or her body pierced.

"What do you think of my job offer?" I ask her.

She hesitates—it's so slight I almost miss it—but I realize its significance. She doesn't want to leave. That's not what she says, though. Instead she lifts her shoulders in a halfhearted shrug and says, "I'll go if you want to go."

It's very brave of her. And when she thinks I'm not noticing I see a line of worry crease her brow. Just like her mother.

"Where's the other surprise?" I think to ask.

Colleen begins to hover around the stove, turning on the oven and the burners. "Oh, in Pap's room," she says nonchalantly.

They've bought a present for him, I guess. Then I hope for no reason at all that it wasn't too terribly expensive. I don't know why I think that. It isn't as if we're hard up. Money goes further in Peabody, and our simpler lifestyle means we don't spend as much. But, still, I can't help but think that whatever they got my father wouldn't be appreciated by him at all. Giving an expensive gift to Pap now would be like giving a Mercedes Benz to a one-year-old.

Colleen and Vicki busy themselves in the kitchen, and I know I'll only get in the way if I stay. I go back to the reception hall for my toolbox, return it to my little "office," and then venture to Pap's room. The door is standing open. I peer in and, just like before, no one is there. Stepping forward, I look around for a present. There isn't anything obvious. I move around the back of the couch to look on the coffee table and suddenly a head pops up, scaring me half to death.

"Hi, Dad," Greg says.

"Good heavens," I say and take a step backwards.

Greg gets to his feet, and I'm astounded by the change in him. Could a few months do so much? He's clean-shaven and tanned, with close-cut hair and an earring in his left ear. He wears a loose shirt, but I can tell he's filled out. His shoulders are broader, and his arms thick with muscles. He has on torn, stained jeans and worn-out work boots. He looks healthier than I could imagine.

He smiles at me nervously.

It would be useless to try to explain the collision of feelings that come. Even as my heart leaps at the sight of my son, even as I want to grab him and pull him close for a hug, even as I believe I should make amends and call it quits on whatever has gone wrong between us, I do none of those things. Somewhere in the pit of my stomach is the feeling that Greg *expects* me to apologize. And why should I? It was Greg who stubbornly left, wasn't it? And so I freeze where I am and say, "He calls me 'Dad.' Is this someone I know?"

A shadow crosses Greg's face.

"Wait," I go on, helpless to stop myself. "Now I remember. You're the world-famous kid who gave up college to—what is it you do? Pump gas? No, that's not it. Sweep up after the horse races? No, that was last spring. Oh—I remember! You're in charge of the french fries at McDonald's. Have you mastered the art of deep-fried, golden-brown yet?"

"I work construction during the day," Greg says with forced politeness. "I work with computers at night. But before you—"

"Construction! Is that where you discovered yourself—or America—or whatever it was you hoped to find? Terrific. I always wanted a son with calluses instead of a college degree."

"Dad, I'm not here to argue. I came to celebrate Pap's birthday."

"Not here to argue?" I challenge him. "That's a shame. I came to argue. It's not like we get to do it much anymore—for as little as we see you."

Greg holds up his hands in resignation. "I quit."

"Meaning what? You'll storm out of here in a tantrum?"

"I wouldn't give you the satisfaction. I'm staying."

"You're staying? Then I'd better notify the Peabody Sentinel." I imagine out loud the headline: "'Greg Reynolds Has Decided to Stay.'"

Greg glares at me.

I glare back, all the while feeling a wash of regret. Why am I being this way? I don't know. But I feel as if I've chosen a path, and I have to stay on it. "Your mother's in the kitchen, if you want to help get ready for the party."

"I'm waiting to see Pap."

"Did you look on the patio?"

"Yes. I think Aunt Minnie took him for a walk."

I'm surprised at this news. The French doors are closed, and I recall that it was ages ago that Minnie took Pap outside.

"Are you sure? Maybe I'd better check the hall," I say and walk to the door.

"I figured out why you're so mad," Greg abruptly says before I can leave.

"Mad?" I ask. "Why should I be mad? What earthly reason would I have for being mad? My only son has forfeited his life to work construction."

"You're not really mad because I haven't gone to college," Greg says.

"I'm not?"

"No. You're mad because I deviated from your plans. I slipped out from under the noose of your control. And it bugs you because I'm *happy*. Did you hear that? I'm *happy*! Let me spell that for you ... H-A-P-P—"

"Don't strain yourself spelling. I wouldn't want you to get calluses on your brain as well as your hands."

Greg folds his arms. I notice he has a small tattoo on one of them. "Admit it. I'm right."

"If I'm mad, it's because I can't stand waste."

"Then you must be especially mad about the twenty years you wasted at the Bradley Company, huh?" Greg says.

"That was *not* wasted!" I shout at him. "It fed you, it put a roof over your head, it put clothes on your back. Don't you dare call my life's work wasted."

"Is that what it was? Your *life's* work? How sad," Greg says. "I thought your *family* was supposed to be your life's work."

I can feel the rage rising through my body like mercury in a thermometer. "I'm not going to stand here to be lectured by you." I'm about to turn on my heel and walk out when Aunt Minnie wheels Pap in from the hall.

Pap complains loudly, "What's all the ruckus? You're making enough noise to wake the dead."

"I hope not," Aunt Minnie says as she closes the doors. "I've got relatives I don't want to see again."

It takes me a moment to understand what Aunt Minnie means. "It's a *joke*, Frank," she half-whispers to me.

Pap sees Greg and holds out his arms, "Greg! Is that you?"

Greg hugs him. "Yeah, it's me, Pap."

Pap gives him hard thumps on the back. "How you been, boy?"

"Fine. Perfect. I can't imagine things being better," Greg says, and I know it's a jab at me.

"How's college?" Pap asks.

I gesture to Greg. "Go ahead. Break his heart."

Greg kneels next to Pap's wheelchair. "I'm not in college, Pap. You know that."

"But you have to go to college," Pap says. "That's where I met your grandmother."

Aunt Minnie rolls her eyes. "Here we go."

"We met in the library, and she was ..." Pap pauses, his brow knitting over his eyes. He looks unsure of himself. "I was on the steps. I sang to her on the steps with a guitar. A song." He looks at Greg, then me, as if he wants us to help him. I open my mouth to speak, but he quickly says, "I don't feel good at all. I want to take a nap."

"Okay, Walter." Aunt Minnie waves us away. "You boys take it into the hallway," she says, then whispers to me, "Dr. McCall?"

I nod and head for the hallway. Greg follows and asks, "How long has he been like this?"

"Like what?"

"Like *that!*"

"You upset him," I say harshly. "First for not going to school, then you come back—"

"Give me a bucket," Greg snaps back. "Why are you acting like this?"

I don't answer, and we walk in silence to the kitchen. I struggle within myself, trying to figure out what could be at work in my life to make me so unpleasant to my son. The questions roll at me, one after another. Do I really resent it that Greg has done something contrary to my plans for him? I try to reject the idea, but it won't go. Other questions follow. Am I upset because Greg left us just as we were heading into the darkest period of our lives? Is that it? Am I dealing with abandonment issues? No, I decide, that's too absurd. Maybe I'm angry because Greg had the audacity to do what I never had the courage to do? I don't know. I honestly don't.

"What do you want, Frank?" I hear Reverend Andy Tyler asking me a few months ago. "What do you *really* want now?"

"I want my old life back," I told him then. And it was true. I wanted my life to be what it was, with everything on course just as I'd expected.

Andy looked at me with an expression of terrible sadness—an expression that haunted me for days after. "Honestly?" he asked. "You don't see anything good about your life now?"

I said, "No. What is there to see?"

"God at work," Andy replied. "Stop and look around you. Stop and listen to your life."

I laughed then, thinking Andy was giving me the old "stop and smell the roses" routine. I'd heard it so many times before from people who seemed to do nothing *but* smell the roses. But now as I walk down the hall with Greg, I realize that Andy might've been talking about something else. Something that Greg has figured out. And it scares me to be left in the dark. Yet the most stubborn part of me clings to my *rightness*, the justification for my anger. *I am right about this*, I know beyond a shadow of a doubt.

"Look, Greg," I say in a conciliatory voice as we enter the kitchen. "All I want is what's best for you."

"No, Dad," Greg counters. "You want what *you want* for me, which may not be the best. Don't you see? You think I'm being foolish, but I've *enjoyed* my life this past year. I've learned a lot."

"I doubt it," I snort.

Colleen at the stove and Vicki at the table now stop what they're doing and look at us. A fluorescent light flickers and buzzes above us. It makes my eyes hurt.

Greg groans at me. "Once—just once—can't you consider a viewpoint other than your own?" He is thoroughly exasperated. I have a petty sense of victory. "You're so . . . so stubborn!" he cries out.

"*I'm* stubborn? *You're* the one who left us high and dry for this ridiculous idea of yours," I shout back at him.

"You gave me an ultimatum, didn't you? Your way or no way, right? Now you harass me for making my choice."

"Because it was the wrong choice," I insist, my voice getting louder.

He is about to shout something back when another voice—high and shrill—suddenly cuts in on our argument. We're both shocked because this voice, one we know so well, is now unrecognizable by its anger.

"Stop it! Stop it right now!" Colleen yells at us. "I'm sick and tired of this fighting. If you want to talk about your differences, then *talk*—but stop this childish bickering! It's tearing me up inside, and I don't want to hear any more of it!"

I stare at her in amazement. So do Greg and Vicki. The face of my wife, one I've known and loved for so many years, is twisted red and splotchy with rage, made all the worse by that flickering fluorescent light. Only once have I ever seen her lose her temper like this. It was a week after her father's funeral, after he lost a long battle against bad health from alcoholism. Colleen had spent hours and hours at the hospital with him, right up to his death, and when they phoned for her to come back to pick up a few of his things, she couldn't bring herself to do it. They phoned two or three times. I didn't understand what was happening with her; it seemed like a simple task. I asked Colleen why she didn't go get her father's things. She wouldn't answer. I pressed the question until she finally shouted, in a red-faced rage, *"I hate hospitals! And never want to set foot in one again!"*

In that moment in the kitchen, I recognize how brave she has been all these months, coming to The Faded Flower with a smile and encouraging words and probably hating it the entire time.

"Colleen...," I say softly.

She is standing by the stove with clenched fists, her body shaking as if it, too, had been scared by her outburst. She turns quickly around to the pan on the stove and begins to stir. Vicki looks at Greg and me with unabashed disapproval.

Greg says quietly, "I'm sorry, Mom. Maybe it was a mistake for me to come." He backs past me out of the door.

I am tempted to say, *There you go, just like always,* but for once I show some restraint. When Greg disappears around the corner, I am also assailed by a tremendous sense of loss, as if I'd been given an important test and failed it.

Vicki approaches Colleen and hugs her from behind. Colleen sighs. Then she hands the spoon to Vicki, tells her to keep stirring, and turns to face me. "When are you going to snap out of this?"

Even her outburst hasn't been enough to shake me loose, and my defenses leap into place. "Snap out of what?"

"Whatever it is that's making you act like this. You're already losing your father. Why do you want to lose your son, too?"

The question is like a cold slap in the face. I'm saved only by Aunt Minnie poking her head around the door. "Did you talk to Dr. McCall?" she asks me.

I had forgotten completely and now move to the phone on the far wall. "I'm sorry. I'll do it right now."

"Is something wrong?" Colleen asks.

"Pap is sick."

Vicki stops her stirring. "Does that mean we can't have the party?"

∞

DR. McCALL, A BAGGY man with large sad eyes and a tiny mouth, confirms that Pap has a fever—102—so it looks like the birthday celebrations will have to be delayed. "As for the cause of the fever, I can't say for sure," he admits. He gives Pap some fever-reducing tablets. "Watch Pap overnight and then, if there's no improvement, call me in the morning."

I'm alone and bewildered as I stand at the foot of my father's bed. He was always a strong, healthy man. Doting over him because of a fever seems overdramatic. But I have to keep reminding myself that his mind and his body are not what they were, we have to take special care of both. The father I knew all those years is nearly gone. He's been replaced by the gray, fragile old man sleeping in front of me with his hands folded over his chest. He could be in a coffin, I think with a shudder.

More than anything, I want to talk to Pap. Well, not *this* Pap, but the one I knew a few years ago. I need some of his advice, a little perspective about my life. I ache to hear him tell me why I'm behaving like such a fool. I don't want to lose my son. I don't want to alienate my family. But a deep anger continues to churn inside of me. "It's eating me alive," I whisper out loud.

But who am I angry with? Maybe Pap, for getting old and becoming so dependent. That's not how it was supposed to be. None of it was. Pap was supposed to be the wise old grandfather, living to a ripe age and then passing on to glory. He wasn't supposed to lose his memory and his bodily functions.

And I was supposed to work at my job until retirement and then play golf and vacation with Colleen. Greg was supposed to go to college and lead a responsible life. Vicki, too. I had it all worked out. It was a good plan, a solid plan. But it went wrong.

I lower my head, and the self-pity makes my eyes water. I feel pathetic and hope to God no one comes in right now.

God. . . I begin to pray, and then stop. I catch something out of the corner of my eye. I glance around the room, certain that someone has come in. No, I'm alone.

"What do you *really* want?" I remember Reverend Andy Tyler asking me.

"I don't know," I whisper. But I'm aware of that *feeling* again. It is a peculiar pain, a longing that I've felt many times before and found myself trying to satisfy or, at the very least, bury so it'll leave me alone.

My father coughs, and I jump. I look up and am surprised to see Pap sitting upright.

"Are you all right? You don't look so good," Pap says.

I'm speechless, very aware that something isn't right. Pap now looks younger somehow. His eyes are alive, and he has that mischievous smile that makes the ends of his lips curl down. He gazes at me. I'm certain that the dim light from the lamp by the bed is playing tricks. Or I'm dreaming.

Pap folds his hands on his lap and asks, "What's on your mind, Son?"

He looks so earnest that I decide to play along with whatever hallucination I'm experiencing. I say to him, "Everything has unraveled, Dad. Everything I've worked for and lived for. It's all gone."

"We've all had better years, I think," Pap says with a genuine smile and I have to blink because Pap's wrinkles and age spots seem to be fading. He's getting younger right before my very eyes. "As for statements like, 'it's all gone'. . . well, I had hoped we raised you better than that."

"What do you mean?"

Pap shakes his head disapprovingly, and I see that his hair is darker.

"Tell me," I plead with him. Even if this is a dream, I want to know what he has to say.

"What did your mother and I teach you?" Pap says sternly. "The Lord's ways are not our ways. He defies our plans because he has better plans for us. You know that."

I sigh. This isn't the revelation I'd hoped for. "Is that the answer?"

Pap leans forward, cupping his upturned knees that make the blanket look like two snow-covered mountains. "You want answers? There are none. The only way to keep your sanity is to hold on as tight as you can to your faith. You have to believe that he knows what he's doing even when you don't. That's all I can tell you, Frank. He loves you. It's easy to think so when things are going the way you want, it's tougher when they aren't."

I look into my father's eyes and am overwhelmed with a feeling of regret.

Pap looks around to make sure no one is listening, then he wiggles a finger at me. "I've realized something."

I circle the bed and sit down next to him. I lower my tone to match his. "What?" I ask.

"It was only a house, you know."

"A house?"

"*My* house. But it wasn't home."

I'm confused. "How can you say that? It was our home for years."

Pap pokes a finger at me. "Not *home*. Only something *like* home." Then he leans towards me and whispers, "Mere reflections, that's all."

I'm still perplexed and reach out to touch his arm. My hand hangs in midair, touching nothing. Then I realize I'm standing back at the foot of the bed, my father still old and gray, deep asleep in front of me.

"I'm losing my mind," I say out loud. And then I think of Spooky Sally and her visions and wonder if God is playing tricks on me.

∞

I GO TO THE Sun Room to put away the folding chairs we'd set up for the party. They aren't needed now. Colleen and Vicki are in the kitchen, wrapping the various goodies for the freezer. Colleen has already announced to everyone that we would have the party when Pap felt better, and Vicki added, "He won't know it's not his birthday anyway."

Before coming to the Sun Room, I lingered awhile in the kitchen, wanting to help, wanting to be near both of the ladies in my life, but they were stiff and formal with me. They didn't want me around—and for good reason.

I knew I should say something to them. I knew I should apologize for what happened with Greg. But I felt too confused. The arrival of that letter, the fight with Greg, my hallucination about Pap . . . everything seemed to tie up my emotions in little knots, like a string of Christmas tree lights. So I came to the Sun Room to get rid of the folding chairs.

Big Band music plays over a portable stereo while I finish my job. It helps me find a rhythm to the folding, lifting, stacking, and folding, lifting, stacking. I wonder if other people hear rhythms like that. I hear them all the time: in the sound of footsteps in a hall, or a dripping tap, or a humming air-conditioner.

"I don't know how you can listen to this stuff," I hear Robert complain to James. They're sitting at their usual table, the only ones left in the large room.

"Then what do *you* want to listen to?" James asks, annoyed.

"Hymns."

James shakes his head. "You can't dance to hymns."

"Some of those newfangled choruses you can."

"Choruses?"

"On overhead projectors."

"Who ever heard of dancing to an overhead projector?" James asks. I put away the last chair and close the closet door.

"I'm talking about the classic hymns in a hymnbook. The ones by great composers like Fanny Crosby."

"Didn't she do 'White Christmas'?"

"You mean *Bing* Crosby, you ninny," Robert explains.

"Don't be silly. Bing Crosby didn't write hymns. He was that comedian."

"What comedian?" Robert asks.

"The black one."

"Black one what?"

"Comedian."

"You mean *Bill Cosby*."

"Is that it?" James muses, then decides it is. "Bill Cosby. He's the one."

Robert scratches his chin. "How odd. I didn't know he wrote hymns."

"As a sideline," James concludes.

Robert slowly stands up and heads for the stereo. "Mind if I turn it off?"

"Yes."

And then the argument starts all over again.

But I don't stay to hear it out.

Lawrence is standing at the door, watching Robert and James with a gentle smile. He looks even more like Stewart Granger in this light, his white hair shining like polished metal. Tipping his head towards the bickering duo, he says, "I sometimes wonder if that's how all of our philosophical and theological discussions sound to God." Before I can respond he asks me, "How's your father?"

"Not well."

He eyes me carefully. "You've had a difficult day."

I try to downplay my answer. "Well, I wouldn't rank it very high, as days go."

"Have some of this," Lawrence says and holds out a cup of something. I look at it suspiciously. Lawrence smiles at me. "It's cider I made for tonight. I'd hate for it to go to waste."

I take the cup and drink. The cider is warm and tangy with a sweet aftertaste. I can't identify the fruit, though. Apples and oranges, maybe. "Pretty good," I say. I can feel the warmth move down my throat to my belly.

"Let's go outside," Lawrence suggests. "It's a beautiful evening."

I follow Lawrence across the Sun Room, glancing back at Robert and James, who've settled down to a game of checkers. Lawrence and I open the large sliding glass door that leads onto the grounds. There is a patio there with a fountain that has been turned into a giant planter. Leaves run around our feet, scooted along by the chilly autumn breeze. It smells like it might snow. I shiver and drain the last of the cider for warmth.

Lawrence sits down on the edge of the fountain and gazes at the sky. I stand where I am and look down at my cup. It seems dark and empty.

"What can I do to help you?" Lawrence asks.

I look at him—or rather, his shadow—and ask, "To help me?"

"There must be something. What do you want?"

Ah, that question again. *What do you want?* "I don't understand," I confess.

Lawrence doesn't say anything for a moment. Then he speaks, and his words feel carefully chosen, as if he's trying very hard to be diplomatic. "I once stood where you're standing. I had an iron grip on my life. I had strategized who I was and where I was going. But it fell apart. I lost my business. My wife left me. I started drinking. I had a heart attack. Every step of the way I thought I could fix whatever had gone wrong, like you fix a hinge on a door or adjust a setting on a furnace. I was wrong. I hit rock-bottom."

I'm surprised by this information. In all the time I've known Lawrence, he has never betrayed his past. I guess I'd always assumed he lived successfully and then simply retired. "And?" I ask, wondering what the punch line could be.

"And when I'd lost everything, I found out what was truly important." He chuckles ironically. "Isn't that how it usually goes? Haven't we all heard the stories of people who have to lose everything to gain perspective? Well, I think it must happen to everyone sooner or later. Only then could I see myself more clearly—I could understand what it was I really wanted. In a way, I came face-to-face with God."

I slump on the rim of the fountain; the cement is cold and clammy. I feel skeptical about this conversation. It sounds too much like a pitch for a pyramid scheme or some testimonial for something that may have worked for him but has nothing to do with me. But politeness demands that I ask, "How did you do all that?"

"*I* didn't do it," Lawrence replies. "It was a conspiracy."

"A what?"

"A conspiracy of grace," Lawrence says. "At least, that's what I call it. Circumstances, coincidences, offhanded comments from friends, strange dreams, guilt, regret . . . I began to see a theme to it all. It was a conspiracy."

"A conspiracy," I mutter. Now I'm really wary and wonder who Lawrence has been talking to. Has he been following me around? How does he know to say these things?

"The whole thing was from God, of course," he says. "Nobody else could have masterminded such a scheme."

"And this conspiracy led you to some great life-changing revelation, is that it?"

"Yes, I suppose it did."

I wait, but Lawrence doesn't say anything else. "Well? Are you going to tell me what it was?"

He shakes his head. "I can tell you, but I'm not sure it'll make sense."

"Try me."

Lawrence pauses long enough to sip some of his cider. "The revelation, if you will, is that we don't belong here."

"Here?"

"In this world," he explains. "We're spiritual nomads, making our way to a final destination. That's why we can't get comfortable here. That's why God won't let us get comfortable. I believe God does things on purpose to remind us that we're not supposed to settle down in this world. That's why we hunger, or yearn, for something that's just beyond our reach."

"I had everything I yearned for," I say. "But God took it away."

Lawrence turns to face me, but I can't see his expression in the shadow. His voice is plaintive. "Did you really think you had everything you yearned for?"

Like a student under the stare of a stern teacher, I flinch. "Well ... yes."

"Well, I'd argue that you were wrong—just like I was. The yearning I'm talking about is for something more permanent, more transcendent, than a job and a house and even a stable family. Those things can be like anesthetics to keep us from feeling the yearning. Do you know what I'm talking about?"

"I'm not trying to be stupid," I say defensively because I *feel* stupid. "But I'm not sure what you're saying." Meanwhile my thoughts leap back to that weird hallucination with my father. Wasn't he saying the same things? Was he part of the conspiracy?

"It's a mysterious ache, an unsettled feeling as if you've forgotten something important or want something terribly but don't even know what it is. It's a joy and sadness all wrapped up in one."

"A longing?" I ask, uneasy that I may actually know what Lawrence is talking about.

Lawrence nods. "Yes. A longing. But I believe that that longing is something God puts inside of us, a longing for eternity. Sometimes it comes in isolated moments, sometimes it comes in a sudden feeling." Lawrence's voice grows softer. "Sometimes it hurts so much that we'll do whatever we can to make it stop. And other times we misunderstand what it is and try to quench it with the wrong things. That's what I did for years."

I fiddle with my cider cup for a moment and then ask, "But what does all this have to do with me?"

In the darkness, I can feel Lawrence's gaze. "I've been watching you ever since you came to work here. You're like a fish caught on a hook, twisting and squirming, desperate to be free. Or, to put it another way, God's got his thumb on you. You've had the hunger, and you've spent most of your life trying to kill it. Why do you think I asked you what you want?"

"I wondered."

"Have you figured out the answer yet?"

I think of all the events of the day, of my confusion and strange behavior, and I honestly have to say, "No."

Lawrence is thoughtful. "Then I wonder what else God is going to have to do to help you find out."

"You make that sound like a threat."

"Let's not be sentimental about it, Frank. God is a loving father—and loving fathers teach their sons, don't they? Even if it hurts sometimes. Isn't that part of the mystery?"

Before I can reply, the sliding glass door opens, and Rose squints in our direction. "Frank?"

"Yes, Rose?"

"Oh, there you are. Your wife is looking for you. Your father is awake, but is terribly confused. She wants you to come to his room."

"All right. Thanks." I stand up. Lawrence does, too. He puts his hand on my shoulder as we walk inside, but he says nothing else.

∞

I ARRIVE AT PAP'S room in time to see Colleen and Vicki struggling to keep Pap in bed. He is fighting to get up.

Colleen says between grunts, "You have to stay in bed."

"The water. Do you hear it?" Pap asks, his voice reflecting some inner alarm.

"Water?" Colleen asks.

"You have to kick the pipes to make it stop," he says.

I go around the bed, and Colleen and Vicki make way. Pap looks awful. His face is pale, his eyes dark. How was it possible that he could have aged so much in only a couple of hours? I put my hand on his shoulder. "We'll take care of it, Dad. I promise."

Pap looks up at me, startled. "What? Who is that?"

"It's me. Frank."

"Frank who?"

Now I'm the one who's startled. He's forgotten a lot of things over the past few months, but never *me*. I look at Colleen for help, but she simply shakes her head. "I'm Frank—your son," I say.

"Oh," Pap says as if he'd rather not argue about it. But then he looks at Vicki. "Do I know who this is?"

"Yes, Pap," she replies. "I'm your granddaughter Vicki."

Pap frowns. "I don't think so."

"Don't be silly. Of course I am." Vicki is unfazed by his lapse of memory.

But I'm not. Something lurches inside of me, like the kind of butterflies you get when the roller coaster suddenly thrusts forward into its first drop. It's fear. A solid fear that time is slipping out from under me. My father is going to die, I realize, and I decide that he can't—he *can't*. There is too much left to resolve.

"Nope. I don't know you," my father says firmly.

"Come on, Dad, don't joke around," I hear myself saying in a small voice. "You know who I am. Please. Think."

Pap turns away. "I can't think. I'm tired. Maybe later."

"No, *now*. Please, Dad."

Colleen puts a hand on my arm. "I don't think he understands."

But I have to persevere. I lean closer to my father's face, so transparent and fragile now. "Dad, please, I want to talk to you."

"No."

"Just look at me and say you know who I am."

Pap won't look at me. He pulls the covers close and says, "I don't know what you're talking about. I'm very tired. Leave me alone." He closes his eyes as if to will a bad dream away.

I linger a moment and then have to surrender. I straighten up. Colleen and Vicki are watchful. "What did the doctor say?" I ask softly.

"He still wants to wait until morning," Colleen answers, then adds quietly, "Memory loss is part of the disease, you know. I read about it. He was going to forget our names sooner or later. It's unnerving, but we have to ignore it."

I'm panicked. I'm convinced he's going to die tonight. Don't ask me why. I suppose it seems like the final punctuation mark to the whole disastrous year. And I think of Lawrence's threat about God having to do something drastic to get my attention. "I want to wait with him," I say.

"All night?" Colleen asks.

"If necessary. You two should go home."

"What about Greg?" asked Vicki.

"Does anyone know where he is?" I ask.

"He came back for the party," Colleen explains. "But when he found out we'd canceled it, he said he might see us at home later." She faces me directly. "Frank, you two have to call a truce."

I nod, only slightly. I can concede that much. My fight with Greg isn't the priority right now. Right now I want to talk to my father. Colleen gives me a quick kiss and leaves. Vicki does the same.

After they leave, I pull up Pap's wingback chair next to the bed and sit down. The room is all shadows to me. Only the light from the bedstand lamp shines, casting a feeble glow. I think of my dream, or the hallucination, from earlier. Pap had looked so much younger then, like the father I knew when I was a boy. I think about that face now and the memories of my childhood come back. They flip past like an album of old black-and-white photos. Pap sitting on a webbed car seat, his armpits ringed with sweat. Pap at a birthday party. Pap holding dripping ice cream cones at the zoo. Pap making breakfast for us all on a Saturday morning. Pap carrying me after a long walk. Pap teaching me to play whiffle ball in the backyard. Pap putting calamine lotion on me after I sat in a patch of poison ivy.

"Turn on my program, will you?" Pap asks.

I realize with a start that he's looking at me. "What?"

"Turn on my program," he says.

My program was what my mother called her favorite soap opera. *Turn on my programs,* she'd say while wiping her hands on her apron. Everything had to stop for her programs. "What program, Dad?"

"On the radio."

I'm afraid he might turn away again if I say there are no programs, so I reach over to the nightstand and push the button on the radio-alarm-clock. A baroque piece of classical music plays. "Is that your program?" I ask.

He closes his eyes without answering.

"Dad," I say, my voice quivering from what I want to say. "I need to talk to you."

"Hmm," he says without opening his eyes.

I go on anyway. "I want to say I'm sorry for making you move out of your house. Maybe you were better off at home. Maybe none of this would have happened if I'd left you alone." Regret is a ball in my throat now. I want to cough. I want to cry, really. "I've botched everything with you, with Greg, with everyone," I confess.

This is ridiculous, I think. Straight from the movies. A deathbed scene with a penitent son. What do I expect, that he'll open his eyes and give me fatherly absolution?

Oh, God, I sure hope so. Hokey or cliched, I don't care. I need one last touch, one last word.

I wait, still hoping.

Pap slowly opens his eyes and looks at me silently.

"I'm sorry, Dad. Do you understand? I'm sorry," I say again, hoping if I'm emphatic enough the words will somehow penetrate the fog around him.

Pap clears his throat. He speaks in a raw, raspy voice. "You need help."

"I guess I do," I admit.

"You should talk to a priest or a doctor. Do you have any family?" he inquires in a voice full of concern.

"Dad, *you're* my family."

Pap raises an eyebrow. "I think you have me confused with someone else." He closes his eyes again. And within a minute, his breathing is rhythmic, loud, and sonorous.

I lean on my knees, hang my head, and cry.

A man with the voice of a funeral director comes on the radio to announce the next piece of music. Barber's *Adagio for Strings*—one of the saddest pieces of music ever written. But I'll accept it as a soundtrack for this pathetic moment in my life.

I sit up straight as the low, melancholic strings play through the tinny speaker. I've missed the moment, I'm sure. And I think, *Isn't that how life is?* You speak too soon, or you hesitate and speak too late and, either way, the moment is gone, the opportunity lost forever—or as good as forever. My timing never was very good for seizing the moment.

And I think of the moments. The moments of longing, of yearning. The moments of innocence and of joy. They come without being beckoned. They can't be controlled. I can't cajole, prod, or fix them. They come and they go, sometimes targeted dead center, other times within sight but just out of reach. They are unpredictable and fickle and even out of place, like laughter at a funeral, or lust in a church service, or silence in a stadium full of people. But however they come and whatever they are, I can't control them.

I can no longer resist that truth. How can I? For all of my efforts to control my life, I still wound up right here, sitting next to a father who doesn't know me, estranged from my son, cut off from my own soul. Someone else has been controlling the events. They've happened on someone else's terms, according to someone else's timetable, not mine.

Lawrence is right. It's a conspiracy, I conclude. And now I relax, slumping into the softness of the chair. It is Pap's favorite chair, and I never understood why. But I do now. The thing is ugly as sin, but so very, very comfortable. If I could close my eyes, just for a minute of rest. . .

"Frank."

I open my eyes again. Was I asleep? I must have been. I'm not sure where I am at first. Pap's room, with the same dim light. Jazz is playing on the radio. The red digits on the clock say it's a few minutes past midnight. Pap is still lying there, but his eyes are open and his expression is serene.

"Yes, Dad?" I ask anxiously. And then I realize he called me by name. "Do you know me, Dad?"

"Kick the pipes, will you?" he says. "They'll wake your mother."

"Yes, Dad. I will."

"Thank you," Pap says. He pulls an arm out from under the blanket and reaches over to pat my hand. "You're a good boy."

"Thanks, Dad."

Pap turns away again and slips into a deep sleep.

I look down at my father's hand, still resting on my own. *This is the moment I want to remember. No matter what happens after this, I want to hold on to this one moment.* And it becomes a prayer.

∞

IT IS 1:30 A.M., and I have the feeling someone is watching me. I'm still in Pap's chair and slowly open my eyes. Pap is lying perfectly still. I lean closer to listen. Is he still breathing? I look at his chest.

The blanket moves almost imperceptibly, up and then down. I'm relieved. I remember when Greg and Vicki were babies; on those days when they had slept much later in the morning than usual, I would slip out of bed on the pretense of going to the bathroom, then would sneak in to make sure the baby was still breathing. Only then could I go back to sleep again.

I gently put my hand on Pap's forehead. It feels normal. The fever must have broken.

Just out of the corner of my eyes I see a shadow move. Greg is sitting on the arm of the couch.

"I didn't know you were there," I say in a half whisper and stretch. I get up and move closer to my son. "Let's go out in the hall. I don't want to wake Pap."

Greg nods and follows me out into the hall. It is empty and dark, except for the electric pseudo-candles every few feet on the wall.

"Have you been here long?" I ask, still whispering.

"I just came in," Greg replies.

Greg's cheeks are rose-colored and his hair is flecked with white. He's wearing an old leather jacket. I dust some of the snow from his shoulders.

"It's snowing," Greg explained. "Just started."

"It's early for snow," I say. "Have you been to the house?"

"I was about to go, but wanted to see how Pap was doing first."

"I think his fever has broken."

"He's not going to die, is he?" Greg asks.

I shrug. "Sooner or later, I guess. But I doubt Dr. McCall thinks it'll happen tonight."

"Good."

There is an awkward silence and I know I have to say something. I crane my neck to look at Pap again, hoping to find some courage. Finally, I say, "Greg, this has been a hard time for us—for me."

"I know. But, listen, Dad—"

I hold up my hand to stop him. "No, please. Let me finish." He waits and I swallow hard. "I'm sorry about everything that's happened. Between us, I mean." My voice is shaking. I could be a teenager back in school.

"No, Dad, *I'm* sorry," Greg say. "I've been acting like a baby."

I shake my head in protest. "It's been me, Greg. You were right about—"

"Really, Dad—"

"Will you listen for a minute?"

"No, I—"

And then we stop and look at one another and have to clamp hands over our mouths to stifle the laughter.

"Are we going to fight over our apologies?" Greg asks.

My throat feels constricted, but I press on. "I want you to know that, no matter what you decide to do, you're my son and I love you, and you're welcome in whatever house we're calling home."

"Thanks."

There's more silence, but it isn't as awkward. I look at my son and want to hug him. But he's got something else on his mind, I can tell. He's tugging at his lower lip, which is his subconscious signal. He always tugs at his lip when he's about to give the punch line of a joke or is about to say something he thinks is important.

"What?" I ask.

He purses his lips. "I'm going back to college in January," he finally says. "I got a student loan."

I hear the words, but I have to check them over to make sure I've heard them right. "Really?"

He nods.

"Well—" I say no more than that because I feel thick and stupid. I don't know how to react. My gut feeling, to be honest, is one of worry that I've badgered him into this decision. "You're not doing it for me, I hope," I eventually say.

"Nope. I've been doing a lot of work with computers, and I realized I've got to get better training. Most companies won't even look at you without a degree." He smiles at me. "I hope you're pleased."

Am I pleased? I move further down the hall, away from the door to keep from disturbing Pap. "I don't know." I have to confess and can hardly believe my own ears at what I'm saying. "College makes sense. But only if you really want to do it." I sound disgustingly reasonable. But I'm sincere.

"I do," he says. "Besides, how else am I going to meet my future wife?"

"Good point."

A nurse I don't know comes down the hall towards us. She looks starched and constrained in her white uniform and gives us both a reprimanding look. She gestures to her watch. "I work here," I explain to her.

"Are you working now?" she asks.

"Well, no."

"Then you're here past visiting hours," she says primly and goes into Pap's room.

"A definite night-shift personality," Greg says.

I'm indignant and follow her in to watch while she checks Pap's vitals. She glares at me, but I refuse to go. We return to the hall, and she looks as if she's going to walk off without saying anything.

"Well?" I ask her.

"His fever has dropped. He seems fine otherwise. Dr. McCall has asked me to keep a special eye on him. So there's no point in all of us crowding him tonight, is there?" She arched an eyebrow as if to answer her own question.

"Let's go home, Dad," Greg says.

I agree, and we head down the hall towards my little office where I keep my things. I put on my coat and pull out some paper in my pocket. It's the letter from Cohen & Marx.

"What's that?" Greg asks.

"An invitation," I reply.

Greg looks at me quizzically.

"Never mind." I shove the letter back into my pocket. "I've lost interest in it."

We step out into the cold night, my son and I. We shove our hands into our coat pockets and hunch our shoulders against the fat flakes of snow that drift and dart like tiny white sparrows. The shops are dark, the bars have red-and-white "Open" signs alight in the smoky windows, cars move slowly by with stiff-armed windshield wipers waving the snow away.

"It should be Christmas," Greg says happily.

"Yeah," I agree. "It feels like it should be Christmas."

Part Three

The End

⊗Pap lay perfectly still while a nurse who looked like a snowman moved slowly around him. Her cold hands touched his forehead and then held his wrist. He tried to hold his breath, thinking that she would leave him alone if he did.

Had that been Frank and Greg near his bed a moment ago? *Was it a moment?* he wondered. Time had become such a blur. Aunt Minnie had taken him for a walk one day. He could still smell the smoke of a wood fire burning somewhere, the leaves were mostly gone from the trees, and the sun looked like a smudge through the clouds. It's going to snow, he had told Minnie. And now look at it, all over his chest and legs. White like a blanket, and nearly as warm, too.

Colleen and Vicki must have been nearby. He could smell Colleen's perfume. Vicki smelled of something sweet, too, but he never figured out what it was. He saw their faces close to his. Their smiles were so reassuring but also so exhausting to him. These days it took a lot of concentration to keep up. But he loved having them around. It was a good thing, all in all, that Frank had lost his job so they could be closer. Family should be together, especially on a cold night like this. Not far away in some foreign land like Dennis always was.

The nurse had won. He simply couldn't hold his breath any longer—and he let go. It was such a long and luxurious breathing out. Almost like sinking into a hot bath in a long tub. The old house had one of those. He remembered how Martha allowed him to soak for a very long time when he came home from the mines. Not one bath, but two. The first bath was to get rid of most of the soot. The second bath was for him to enjoy. She brought him a cup of coffee and knelt next to him to tell of the day's events and everything the boys had been up to.

It was so warm under his blanket, and he could feel the weight of it on his chest as he exhaled. It pressed down, helping him to let go. He didn't think he had so much breath in his body to release. But there it went, swirling away from him in little eddies.

He felt a hand in his, but kept his eyes closed. Was it that nurse? No, the hand was too warm. It could have been the hand of Frank, with his long, slender fingers—just like Martha's. The hand squeezed his, and his mind was filled with memories of the touch: holding hands with Martha, helping her out of the car, pulling her up from her garden work, taking the little hands of his boys as they crossed the street, holding their hands in his as he showed them how to swing a bat, shaking their hands as young men. A million moments of the slightest touches, and they all came back to him now. Then the hand tugged at him gently, drawing him out like Martha had so often done at the end of his hot bath in the long tub.

His breath was almost gone now. Why, it was such a feeling of purity, of cleansing, that he wasn't sure he wanted to breathe in ever again.